W9-CBU-140

FINDING THE BEST FRIEND OF HIS LIFE

Turning back toward the water, Allan stared in disbelief. He had wished for a dog, and as though some good fairy had waved a magic wand, there *was* a dog.

The dog looked like a big Labrador retriever, but with a mixture of some other breed. Its coat was dull black, and seemed matted and unkempt.

Allan watched the retriever with rising excitement. The dog was on thin ice but apparently aware of its precarious situation. It walked slowly, keeping in a straight line. By itself that was not unusual; all experienced dogs know how to handle themselves in dangerous places. But every few feet this dog left a splash of bright blood. It was hurt, perhaps badly hurt, but even so it seemed to have every intention of retrieving the wing-tipped mallard.

Allan held perfectly still, until it seemed to him that his breathing was unnecessarily loud. A shout, a cry, might frighten the big animal and bring him to disaster.

Then the ice broke, and the dog was in the water. . . .

WITHDRAWN
LVC BISHOP LIBRARY

ALSO BY JIM KJELGAARD

WITHDRAWN

LVC BISHOP LIBRARY

Stormy

by Jim Kjelgaard

A DELL YEARLING BOOK

35 Years of Exceptional Reading

Dell Yearling Books
Established 1966

Published by
Dell Yearling
an imprint of
Random House Children's Books
a division of Random House, Inc.
1540 Broadway
New York, New York 10036

If you purchased this book without a cover you should be aware that this book is stolen property. It was reported as "unsold and destroyed" to the publisher and neither the author nor the publisher has received any payment for this "stripped book."

Text copyright © 1959 by Jim Kjelgaard
Cover art copyright © 1986 by Bantam Books

All rights reserved. No part of this book may be reproduced or transmitted in any form or by any means, electronic or mechanical, including photocopying, recording, or by any information storage and retrieval system, without the written permission of the Publisher, except where permitted by law. For information address Holiday House, Inc., 425 Madison Avenue, New York, New York 10017.

The trademarks Yearling® and Dell® are registered in the U.S. Patent and Trademark Office and in other countries.

Visit us on the Web! www.randomhouse.com/kids

**Educators and librarians, for a variety of teaching tools, visit us at
www.randomhouse.com/teachers**

ISBN: 0-553-15468-0

Reprinted by arrangement with Holiday House, Inc.

Printed in the United States of America

First Yearling edition December 2001

30 29

CWO

To
Mike and Gertie Stempfhuber

Table of Contents

1. Treacherous Ice

Allan Marley glanced out of the window at a cloudy, threatening sky. The mid-November twilight was stealing over this north country, where spring and summer and autumn were pleasant but brief, and all the rest was winter. In spite of gathering darkness, he decided that there was time to go look again at the wing-tipped mallard.

Allan slipped into his hunting jacket, a lined-wool, belt-length garment that allowed freedom of movement and at the same time shielded him from the bitter wind. He put on a woolen cap, turned the ear flaps down, and pulled mittens over his hands. When he opened the door, the wind almost snatched it from his hand. He bent his head to the blast and walked toward the lake.

The sycamores and oaks that surrounded his house were bending before the wind. Dried leaves, snatched from parent branches, were whisked high into the air and out of sight. Lowering clouds forecast more snow to be added to the eight inches already on the ground. Following the path by instinct, Allan came to the lake's edge, raised his head, and saw the mallard drake.

Save for a very small area in the center, the lake wore an armor of glistening ice. In the tiny patch of water remaining in the center, the mallard was paddling continuously, and always in a circle, in a desperate attempt to keep that water from freezing over. It was a losing battle. At noon the circle of water had been perhaps fifteen feet in diameter; now it had narrowed to less than eight. Within the next couple of hours, the frigid blasts screaming out of the north would close it completely.

Allan frowned. He himself assiduously hunted the ducks and geese that winged down this flyway every autumn. Far from suffering twinges of conscience when he tumbled a teal, gadwall, or pintail out of the air, he knew waterfowl shooting as the finest of sport. But that a duck should suffer a lingering death while the ice closed in was something else again.

He was sure that the drake had not been injured on this lake; rarely did anyone except Allan shoot here now and he had left no cripples so far this year. The mallard must have been shot from some other blind, soared this far before tumbling, and been unable to take to the air again. But it was here now, and that made it Allan's responsibility.

He placed an exploring foot on the ice, and when it did not break, he put his other foot beside it. There was an ominous yielding as the ice sank; radial cracks spread and water seeped through them. Allan drew hastily back. The ice still wasn't thick enough. If he tried to walk out on it, he would almost surely fall through. He stood still a moment, wondering what to do.

The ice was too thin to bear his weight and too thick to break with one of the light Marley skiffs. The mallard was hopelessly beyond shotgun range and a near-impossible target for a rifle; otherwise he could shoot it and save it from a slow death from the encroaching ice. A retriever, unaffected by icy water and zero temperatures because of its thick coat, might be able to get the drake. But though Allan had always wanted such a dog, he had none of any kind.

Allan knew that the drake's fate was a part of nature. The hurt or afflicted that cannot cure themselves must die, and nature is indifferent as to how much suffering they endure before death relieves them. But he had a deep-seated and inborn love for the strong-winged, far-journeying waterfowl that came down this flyway every autumn and went up it every spring. Though he knew of no way to aid the hurt mallard, neither could he leave it.

The wind began to keen louder than ever. A heavy branch, torn from a dying sycamore on the very edge of the lake, fell on the ice, cracked it, and water bubbled up. The wind would probably die with nightfall and by morning the ice would bear Allan's weight. But by morning the drake would be dead, frozen in the ice. As though he might find an answer there, Allan turned to look back toward the house.

It was snugly built and well insulated, with one long wing given wholly to bunks and lockers. It was there that the waterfowl sportsmen had slept, those hunters whom Allan and his father had guided, and who had furnished most of their livelihood. But that was before Allan's father had argued with crusty old Bert Torrance, and had beaten him so savagely that Bert was laid up a full month in the hospital. For the past twelve months, with eighteen more to go, Bill Marley had been eating his heart out in the prison at Laceyville. Assault with intent to kill, they had called it.

Some of Bill Marley's friends still muttered that the sentence was far out of proportion to the crime. But when he imposed it, Judge Bender had reminded Allan's father that it was his sixth offense in four years, that he'd had ample warnings, and that prison would offer an opportunity to meditate on the virtues of keeping one's temper. Now the sportsmen did not come, and Allan lived alone.

Turning back toward the water, Allan stared in disbelief.

He had wished for a dog, and as though some good fairy had waved a magic wand, there *was* a dog. Evidently it had emerged from the brush and woods to Allan's left. When he first saw it, it was about a hundred yards out on the lake.

The dog looked like a big Labrador retriever, but with a mixture of some other breed. Its head was too long and its muzzle too slim for a retriever, as though somewhere in its ancestry an infusion of collie or German shepherd had crept in. Its coat was dull black, and seemed to be matted and unkempt.

Allan watched the retriever with rising excitement. The dog was on thin ice but apparently wholly aware of its precarious situation. It walked slowly, keeping in a straight line and doing nothing that might aggravate its already perilous position. By itself that was not unusual; all experienced dogs know how to handle themselves in dangerous places. But every few feet this dog left a splash of bright blood. It was hurt, perhaps badly hurt, but even so it seemed to have every intention of retrieving the wing-tipped mallard.

Allan held perfectly still, until it seemed to him that his breathing was unnecessarily loud. A shout, a cry, might disconcert the big animal and bring him to disaster. Then the ice broke and the dog was in the water.

The ice had given way because the lake had frozen from the edges to the middle, and the nearer the dog came to the mallard, the thinner the ice upon which it walked. But the retriever handled itself like a master, with no strength-wasting surging or splashing. It did not turn back, but went steadily on toward its quarry. When it tried to climb out on the ice the thin film broke beneath the dog, and thereafter the retriever continued to break through with its own weight while it continued toward the wing-tipped drake. However, the dog was hurt, as had been proved by blood left on the ice, and now it seemed to be weakening.

Allan turned and ran back to the house. He drew a pair of long one-by-eights from a pile of weathered lumber, shouldered them, and ran back toward the lake. He saw that the dog had meantime overtaken and seized the drake and was headed back to shore. But each time it tried to climb onto the ice, the only possible avenue of escape, its weight broke the ice and dropped the retriever back into the water. After several tries the dog rested, only its head showing, then tried again and broke through the ice again.

Allan unbuttoned his jacket, threw it down, and did not even feel the wind's bite as he knelt to unlace and pull off his rubber pacs. He loosened his belt, slid his hunting pants down, kicked them beside the jacket, and then shed his wool shirt. Dressed only in underwear and socks, he laid his two boards side by side on the ice. Every impulse urged him to hurry and help the dog, but he knew too much about the ice to let himself rush into any unwise move. Lightly clad though he was, if he fell through he would have real trouble getting out.

With one foot on each board, he walked slowly onto the ice and felt it yield beneath his weight. When he reached the ends of the boards, he halted and stepped carefully from one to the other. Moving his feet as little as possible in order to create a minimum of disturbance on the ice, he knelt to slide the unencumbered board ahead of him, stepped onto it, and pushed the other board up beside its mate. Moving one board at a time, he continued his slow progress toward the trapped dog.

Reason told Allan that this was a foolish thing to do, and that he himself might drown in what could prove a vain attempt to rescue a strange dog. But he did not turn back. This was the flyway upon which he lived, and upon which his father and grandfather before him had lived. The flyway and the waterfowl that had made it their north-south highway for ages past were as much a part of him as the blood that nourished his body. Out on the ice a great dog that also belonged to this kind of life was in desperate trouble and there was only one solution. He must help.

Raising his head, Allan saw the dog, still a long way out and still trying to climb onto the ice. But the attempts were more feeble now and the rests much longer. Allan returned his attention to what he himself was doing. Knowing that any attempt to hurry, or any slight miscalculation, would bring certain failure and possible tragedy, Allan restrained his impatience and fought himself into making progress the slow but sure way. Stepping from one board to the other when he reached their ends, then pushing both ahead of him, he continued toward the center of the lake. As he came to thinner and thinner ice, the whole ice sheet dipped, and here and there water seeped through a fissure or bubbled through an air hole. Allan walked slowly on.

A scattering of snow fell, and a gusty burst of wind whirled the flakes across the ice in a twisting snow devil. Allan looked up at the darkening sky. Winter in the Beaver Flowage was always harsh, with deep snow, bitter winds, and zero temperatures the rule rather than the exception. But at sporadic intervals occurred what was known locally as a black storm, so called because snow fell so thickly that even high noon turned to black night, and landmarks were wholly blotted out. As he made his way toward the dog, Allan knew that a black storm was in the making. If it built up fast enough to catch him while he was still on the ice, only the greatest of good luck would get either him or the dog back to shore.

But if he turned back now, the dog was surely doomed. Allan stubbornly pushed and pulled his boards along, until he suddenly saw open water ahead.

The dog was now saving its remaining strength just to keep its head above water, but Allan noted with a rising thrill that the mallard remained in its mouth. Allan had only a passing glance for the dog itself, but it was enough to note the deep intelligence in the retriever's eyes. This was confirmed when the dog turned weakly to swim toward Allan. Help was at hand and the big animal knew it.

Lying full length on his boards, Allan stretched a hand as far as he could reach and felt for a collar. Finding none, he grasped the slack skin on the retriever's neck and, while the dog helped itself by pawing, succeeded in drawing it out of the water to a point where the ice held. The dog staggered, almost went down, then righted itself and placed the mallard, that had scarcely a ruffled feather, in Allan's hand. Allan tucked the wing-tipped drake under his arm and looked at the dog closely.

As he had thought when he had first seen it, it was big, but thin to the point of emaciation. The wound was in its right side. Obviously the immersion in ice water had lessened the flow of blood; only a trickle stained the black fur now. The dog staggered again, took a dizzy step, and saved itself from falling by stiffening its legs. A starvation diet combined with the wound had brought about extreme weakness, Allan realized. Even so, the dog had shown itself a superb retriever and now proved that it had the heart to go with the ability. Courage alone was keeping the animal on its feet.

Allan turned and, keeping anxious eyes on the dog, started moving his boards back toward the shore, the mallard still tucked under his arm. Near collapse, but forcing itself to walk, the dog padded slowly along about three feet to one side. As they moved on to firmer ice, the storm increased in fury. Wind-driven snow pellets stung Allan's cheeks and falling snow combined with deepening night to make the shore line almost invisible. Allan set his course toward his house, a blurred shape in the storm and gathering darkness.

At last they reached the shore. The dog scrambled up the bank, then its legs collapsed, and it fell in a tumbled heap.

Knowing he must hurry but fighting panic, Allan slipped his feet into the discarded pacs, tucked the wing-tipped drake beneath a copse of brush where it huddled motionless, and knelt to slip his arms under the dog's chest and hind quarters. As he lifted the dog, Allan gave a grunt of surprise. An adult Labrador should weigh about sixty-five pounds, but despite its gauntness, this dog was heavier. Cradling the animal in both arms, Allan trotted to the house, pushed the door open with his knee, and laid the inert dog gently beside the stove.

As he straightened up, Allan was aware for the first time of the effects of his having gone out on the ice wearing only underwear and socks. His whole body was numbed with cold, and before he could do anything else, it was imperative to get warm. He fumbled at the stove door, and had to use both hands to open it. He placed a chunk of wood on top of glowing coals, watched it blaze, and stood over the stove until feeling returned to his numbed hands. Then he turned for his first unhurried examination of the dog.

It was even bigger than it had seemed at first glance, at least a third larger than any retriever Allan had ever seen, with some odd strain added. Allan decided after a close scrutiny that the tempering strain was neither collie nor German shepherd but some rangier dog such as a staghound or wolfhound. Save for a very narrow semi-oval of white around the base of the neck, the dog's fur was dull black like a Labrador's and at the same time had a Chesapeake's curl. It was badly matted and burr-ridden, betraying lack of care. From a flesh wound on the right side blood was dribbling to the floor.

Warm enough now to move freely, Allan put a dish of water over the hot lid of his wood-burning stove. When the water started to bubble, he dropped in a large needle and a pair of surgical scissors. He had used them both before. On occasion, especially in winter when snowbound residents of the Beaver Flowage could not get out and doctors were unable to get in, the wilderness dwellers had taken care of their own hurts and ills.

As he waited for his instruments to sterilize, Allan looked at the big animal thoughtfully. It was a foregone conclusion that any dog capable of sighting a wing-tipped mallard at the distance this one had, and of retrieving so skillfully, had had considerable and expert training. The dog was a mongrel, or at least had no pedigree. But some hunters, finding a mutt with promise, would lavish as much attention on it as they would on any dog whose heart pumped only the bluest of blood. No hunter, unless he was one of the very few who thought a dog worthless unless pedigreed, would lightly relinquish a retriever such as this. It therefore followed that sooner or later someone would come to claim the animal he had saved.

Allan knelt beside the dog, parted its black hair, and to his astonishment looked down on a bullet hole. The slug, apparently a 30-30 or similar, had struck the lower right ribs and plowed inward. Since there was no wound where the bullet had emerged, it was still there and must be taken out.

Allan rummaged through a miscellany in a drawer and found two crochet hooks that had belonged to his mother. He dropped them into his pan of boiling water. While they were sterilizing, he knelt to cut all the hair away from the wound, then fished out the sterilized crochet hooks. As he probed, the dog wriggled, grunted, and twitched its paws. Allan withdrew his probe until the big animal quieted, then resumed working. The crochet hook slid past splintered bone to stop at the imbedded slug. It was not as deep as Allan had feared it would be.

Allan worked out a soft-nosed bullet that had miraculously failed to mushroom. Probably both that failure and the bullet's not going clear through were explainable by the fact that it had been shot at very long range, and doubtless the dog owed his life to that circumstance. Allan disinfected the wound, sewed it with silk thread because he lacked surgical gut, then stood up and looked at the dog with a puzzled frown.

Some retrievers are worthless, some fair, some good, and a few grand indeed. But would the best among them, the truest champion with the stoutest heart, even try to retrieve a duck from icy water if he had a bullet in his ribs? There was an enigma here, one that offered no pat solution. Only a waterfowl hunter who both loved and understood dogs could have owned this one. What was the dog doing here? And who had shot it, and why?

The dog's paws twitched and a rippling shudder passed over its ribs. The big jaws opened and shut, then the retriever raised its head and looked squarely at Allan. In the look was a certain quality that was not untamed, but wild in the same sense that an unrestricted hawk or swan is wild. To humans who themselves had drawn so far from things elemental that they no longer understood or even recognized it, it could be entirely savage. But Allan, born to the flyway, warmed to it. His cradle song had been the cry of the wild geese winging north. He knew the vocabulary of the ducks, from their cries of alarm to their rallying and mating calls, and he sympathized with the urgings that sent them on their far-flung journeys. Just so, in spite of its outward wildness, he understood this dog.

When Allan extended a hand, the dog neither flinched nor made any attempt to meet the hand.

"I don't know where you came from, fella," Allan

said gently, "but I hope you stay with me. While you do, your name is Stormy. Now you lie right there; I'll be back soon."

Allan pulled on another pair of hunting pants, put on a parka coat, and set a lighted lantern in the window. Then he picked up a flashlight and went back into the night. The wind was still blowing, and wind-driven snow battered the house. Allan ran back down to where he had shucked his clothing, gathered it up, and flashed his light under the copse of brush where he had left the wing-tipped mallard. To his surprise, the drake was still huddled there, too confused or too exhausted to have moved away. Allan picked it up, and, guiding himself by the lantern in the window, ran back toward the house. He stopped long enough to put the mallard in a weather-proof shed before going back to the dog.

Stormy was lying quietly and merely turned a steady gaze on Allan as he came in. There was no hostility in the gaze. But neither was there any overt friendliness; this dog had no intention of fawning upon him, that was sure. Allan grinned.

"All right, all right; be stand-offish. But I reckon you can use something to eat. You'll get it as soon as I slick up a mite."

He had just started to wipe up the blood the dog had spilled, when he had a sudden recollection. He caught up some old editions of the *Tillotson Courier*, the local weekly that he always saved and, sooner or later, always used. He shuffled through them, and on the third paper from the bottom found what he wanted. There was a picture of a dog, the same one that now lay on his floor. The accompanying headline and story read:

OUTLAW DOG AT LARGE!

Cardsville, Oct. 16. Entirely without warning a huge crossbreed dog, formerly the property of Del Crossman, of Gull Lake, but for the past month living on the Zermeich farm, attacked Jacob Zermeich early this morning. After beating the animal off with a pick handle, Zermeich, who suffered severe lacerations, called Deputy Burmeister. A posse found no trace of the dog, which is thought to be rabid and should be shot on sight.

Allan lowered the paper, glanced at the dog, and looked back at the picture. He had no doubt that this was the same animal. That it had belonged to old Del Crossman, a renowned woodsman and duck hunter who had died some two months ago, explained its hunting skill. It was not and never had been rabid, or it would have been dead weeks ago. But why had it attacked a human being, what was it doing here, more than fifty miles from the scene of that attack, and who had shot it? The paper dangling from his hand, Allan looked steadily at the dog, thinking.

When Allan came forward again, Stormy made no move to retreat but neither was there any friendly wag of the tail. The dog was very alert, as though to anticipate the next move of this man and be ready for it. When Allan stooped to wipe the floor, Stormy sniffed his hand.

Allan threw the bloody paper into the stove and opened two cans of beef soup. Then, recklessly, he added two more, dumped all of them into a kettle, and put the kettle over to warm. When the soup was hot enough, Allan poured it into another dish and put it on the floor.

Stiffly, but without apparent pain, the dog rose and sniffed. Then, in spite of what must be raging hunger, Stormy ate slowly and with dignity. Finished, and with no trace of weakness or unsteadiness now, the retriever walked to the far wall and lay down again.

Smiling to himself, Allan prepared his own supper.

2. TILLOTSON

Next morning's thin, pale dawn was dim against the frosted windows when Allan awoke. For a few minutes he lay drowsily in bed, savoring the warmth of his quilts and reluctant to leave them. Then he leaped out, ran to the stove, and poked beneath gray ashes until he found hot coals. Adding wood, he raced back to bed. He noted in passing that the water pails, standing on a bench beside the door, had a skim of ice on them.

Still lying against the far wall, Stormy raised his head and soberly watched Allan's activity. It was much colder where the big dog had slept than it would have been by the stove, but most retrievers didn't mind cold. Allan remembered that John Deerfield, a Tillotson guide who owned two fine Chesapeakes, had built a wall of snow to protect their kennels from the bitter winds. Scorning both kennels and windbreak, the dogs had chosen to sleep on top of the wall even in below-zero weather.

The fresh wood began to crackle and the stove's welcome warmth spread through the room. Twenty minutes later Allan left his bed a second time, carried his clothing to the stove, and dressed beside it. Remaining reserved and aloof, Stormy followed him with his eyes. As he buttoned a wool shirt over long woolen underwear, it occurred to Allan that Stormy might have been mistreated by human beings to such an extent that he no longer had confidence in them.

Allan pulled on rubber-bottomed, leather-topped pacs, laced them, and went to the front window. He used his forefinger to melt a hole in the frost-rimed glass and saw by the thermometer attached to the outside sill that it was twenty-seven below. That was cold but not unbearable, and certainly the lake ice would now support almost anything that ventured onto it. Snow must have fallen furiously during the night, for drifts up to six feet deep had formed wherever there was enough of an obstruction to stop the wind-driven snow. In other places there was only frozen brown earth.

Looking through his peephole again, Allan saw that the lake ice had been swept clean by the wind. Along the shore a few willow withes thrust above the ice. They marked the places where muskrats grubbed for succulent roots and bulbs. Allan trapped muskrats in late winter and early spring, when pelts were at their best. If next spring's breakup was late, it would be necessary to trap beneath the ice, and the willows would show him where to do it.

A flock of pert chickadees, heads to the wind that still blew, were lined up on a single branch of a leafless maple. Allan smiled at the sight. Chickadees, scarcely bigger than a puff of thistledown, seemed to start assuring each other as soon as the first autumn frost whitened the ground that spring couldn't possibly be far behind. Nor did the most severe blizzard ever seem to daunt them.

Allan glanced once more at the undulating, uneven blanket of snow. Usually the wind died at night and usually, too, there was no snow when it was this cold. Last night's storm had been an exception on both counts.

Allan used all his remaining flour to prepare a bowl of flapjack batter. He put his griddle on, let it heat, greased it, poured flapjacks on, and fed the dog before he himself ate. Although obviously hungry, the big retriever again ate in a dignified, leisurely way. Definitely a mongrel, Stormy still had a courtliness and grace that set him apart. He was as sure of himself as a healthy tiger at a kill, and Allan found himself hoping that he might keep this wonderful hunter for his own.

Allan ate his own breakfast and washed the dishes. When he put on his wool cap and jacket, Stormy looked expectantly up and crowded to the door. Allan hesitated. Stormy should go out, but if he did he might leave. It would be better to clean up the floor than to take any chances.

"Stay!" Allan said sharply.

With no indication that he had even heard, Stormy continued to wait anxiously for the door to open. Allan frowned. Anyone able to teach a dog to hunt as this one could should certainly have taught it manners too.

"Down!" Allan ordered.

When Stormy refused to lie down, Allan opened

the door just enough to let himself slip through. Even so he had to push the dog back with his knee. Now he was even more puzzled. Retrievers must often travel in boats, and if they refuse to lie still on command they might very well endanger both the boat and its occupants. They are also hunted from blinds, and those that move about when ordered to lie still would surely frighten waterfowl that might otherwise come within range of the gunners.

The answer must be that Stormy was a one-man dog. He hunted because he loved to hunt, but had never considered himself obliged to obey anyone except old Del Crossman. And Del was dead.

Allan took his toboggan from its rack behind the house, tied his snowshoes to it, and looped a quantity of quarter-inch rope through one of the toboggan's struts. These winter trips to Tillotson, when he could pull a whole load of supplies, did not have to be made nearly as often as in summer, when he must back-pack everything he wanted.

Finally Allan went to the shed where he'd left the wing-tipped mallard. It was standing quietly in a corner, not liking these strange surroundings. When Allan bent to seize it, it darted away. It was cornered on the third try, and after a few protesting flaps of its wings, placed in a wooden box. Allan nailed slats over the box, lashed it to the toboggan, and started up the ice.

He did not need snowshoes here, for last night's high wind had whipped all snow from the ice. Now the wind had lulled to little more than a breeze, and the below-zero cold only made his cheeks tingle pleasantly. Chickadees in the willows along the shore line twittered cheerfully and a great horned owl flapped a slow way across the lake. Unconsciously Allan noted the copse of trees in which the big bird disappeared. Great horned owls were predators but they were not, in Allan's view, pests to be exterminated at all costs. Among their uses were keeping rodents in check, removing diseased creatures that might infect others, and killing injured ones that otherwise would certainly suffer a lingering death.

When a single mottled feather blew across the ice in front of him, Allan halted in his tracks. Then, leaving his toboggan, he followed the wind to the shore, passed through a fringe of willows, and came upon a scattered mass of feathers clinging to a grove of knee-high hemlocks. An incautious grouse had roosted in these little trees and a prowling mink had caught it. Allan marked this place, for he wanted to trap the mink. Far-roaming creatures, mink establish and cling to pretty much the same beat. Perhaps in one week and perhaps not for two or more, this one would come back to the hemlocks. It could be lured into them, and the trap Allan would have ready, by scent.

A half-mile up the ice Allan came to a wide path. This was a public freeway which must at all times be open to anyone wanting to reach this lake. He took his snowshoes from the toboggan, harnessed them to his pacs, and began trampling down a shoulder-high drift. A few minutes later he succeeded in breaking a path for his toboggan. There followed a short space with little snow, then drifts deeper than the first. At the end of forty-five minutes' hard work, Allan stood on the border of Torrance land.

He looked out on wide, cleared acres, with here snow drifts, there stubble thrusting like brown knitting needles through places where the snow had blown shallow, and in the distance a comfortable house, huge barn, and snug outbuildings. The Marleys owned the more than a thousand acres of cutover timber and marshland around the lake, but the Torrances owned everything on this side that led to civilization. There had been a time when Torrances and Marleys trespassed on each other's property with never a thought save that they were welcome. But no longer, Allan thought bitterly.

William Marley had never wanted a farm. He had been born to the lake and the ways of the wild creatures that lived on and around the lake, and there had been no better or more famous waterfowl guide in the whole Beaver Flowage. Sportsmen travelled halfway across a continent to hunt with Bill Marley. Long before the season officially opened, Marley Lodge had as many reservations as it could handle, and Allan and his father had boarded and guided the hunters. The very fields upon which Allan now looked had held goose pits, from which Marley clients shot wary geese that came to glean the fallen grain.

Then came the quarrel, and like most such it overlapped the ridiculous. Bert Torrance and Bill Marley had shot at the same duck and both had claimed it. Both proud of their marksmanship, neither was especially interested in the duck and would gladly have relinquished it to the other, but under no circumstances would either admit that the other had killed it. What started as a spirited argument led to hot words. With the first blow Bill Marley's touchy temper had exploded and he had beaten the older man senseless.

Allan went soberly on. That had happened only a short year ago, but it seemed another day and age when happy hunters who overflowed the bunk room at Marley Lodge had driven their cars down a road that crossed this farm of Joe Torrance, Bert's oldest son. After the quarrel, the Torrances saw to it that there were no more cars. Even though state law decreed that there must be public access to the lake, it didn't necessarily have to be a road and Joe Torrance had closed it down to a footpath. Thus the beginning of the inevitable end. Hunters who could find good shooting in more accessible places were not inclined to indulge in any unnecessary walking. With his father in prison and the road shrunk to a path, Allan hadn't had a single waterfowl hunter to guide last fall. He could, and did, shoot for his own table, which helped out his meager resources, but that was all.

There was a little money Bill Marley had saved, but Allan used this sparingly and supplemented it by trapping furs and working at any odd jobs he was able to get. There was never an abundance of these and such as Allan was able to find did not pay well. The Torrances, all-powerful in the Beaver Flowage, saw to that.

As he pulled his toboggan across the Torrance farm, Allan tried to keep from his mind the thought that, in the not too-distant future, he would no longer be going to Tillotson. His money had melted away far more swiftly than he'd thought possible; at the best, trapping was a precarious existence. Depending on how much fur he took, he might last through next waterfowl season and into the following summer. Unless he could somehow manage to get hunters back, he couldn't possibly hold on longer than that.

Joe Torrance's shaggy farm dog, in due performance of its duty, barked at him in a half-hearted fashion, and someone emerged from the house to see why the dog was making such a noise. Allan hurried. One Marley who couldn't control his temper was one too many, and Allan wanted no more quarrels.

He reached the highway, that had been transformed into a miniature canyon by heaps of snow that the plows had thrown to either side, removed his snowshoes, and strapped them on the toboggan. A half-hour later he was in Tillotson.

Typical of most vacation villages, in summer and throughout waterfowl season Tillotson buzzed with activity. Cars from many states parked on its streets, its stores were crowded, and conversation ran high over some fisherman who had taken a huge pike or some hunter who, in an unusual fashion, had distinguished himself duck hunting. In winter, when all who could afford it went to loaf in some sunnier clime and many who could not went to work in southern resorts or hotels, Tillotson became the stronghold of a few dozen hardy souls who liked cold weather and a few hundred of the less hardy who would have liked to leave but were kept in this semi-arctic region by their work.

The side of town from which Allan entered was devoted exclusively to motels. Here, in season, rooms were at a premium and rates according. Re-membering the twenty-seven below he had read on his thermometer earlier that morning, Allan grinned as he noted the name on one of the closed motels. It was Kool-Aire.

Allan swerved up a side street to a neat white house with a double garage behind it. Blue smoke curled out of the house's chimney to mingle thinly with the cold air. Drifts had piled against one side of the house, and the storm windows were partly frosted. This was the home of Jeff Darnley, game warden for the Beaver Flowage. Jeff himself opened the door when Allan knocked.

"Hello, Al."

"Good morning, Jeff." Allan nodded toward the box on his toboggan. "I've got a wing-tipped mallard drake for you."

Jeff said plaintively, "On a morning like this you bring me a shot-up duck! Come on in!"

Allan grinned as he entered the living room. He greeted Doris, Jeff's pretty wife, then turned to the warden. Weighing not more than a hundred and forty pounds in his winter clothing and pacs, Jeff's lack of stature and seeming lack of strength had proved the downfall of more than one game-law violator who had elected to try conclusions with him. Winded like a greyhound and supple as a mink, Jeff packed the wallop of a ten-pound maul in either fist. He also complained about anything and everything, but he wouldn't have changed jobs for five times his present modest salary. Jeff Darnley was far and away the best warden ever to patrol this area.

"The drake was out in the lake," Allan explained. "He was trying to keep a little puddle open and—"

"Why didn't you leave him?" the warden snapped. "There must be five hundred crippled ducks frozen in one lake or another."

"Yeah. I suppose so. But—"

"Why didn't you just wring his neck if you had to pull him out of the lake?" the fiery little warden asked. "Then the least you'd have had is a duck dinner and nobody would have been the wiser."

"Me?" Allan asked solemnly. "Hurt a pore lil' duck?"

Jeff grinned. Waterfowl season had been closed for the past two days, and might as well have been for the past ten since an early winter had sent most ducks and geese south anyway. The wing-tipped drake would now go to the State Experimental Station at Darville, where it would presumably spend the rest of its life siring more mallards.

"Is it badly hurt?" Jeff asked.

"Just enough so it can't fly."

"Well, leave it in the garage and I'll take it down to Darville."

"Have a cup of coffee, Allan?" Jeff's wife asked.

"I was hoping you'd say that, Mrs. Darnley."

She brought two cups of coffee and Allan and Jeff sipped gingerly of the scalding brew.

"Seen anything of a big killer dog out your way?" Jeff asked seriously.

"Killer dog?" Allan's heart sank.

"Yeah. A mongrel darn near the size of a horse, and he's a man killer. He tackled a man up at Cardsville, fellow named Zermeich, and might have done him in if Zermeich hadn't beaten him off with a pick handle. Only one man's had a good look at him since."

"Who was that?"

"Deputy Sheriff Bill Tarbox had one long shot with a 30-30 about twenty miles north of Tillotson. That was a week ago and Bill thinks he connected but can't be sure; there was no blood. Providing he's still alive, that dog's a bad one to have loose, so just shoot if you see him. You can't make a mistake. The dog has a lot of both Labrador and Chesapeake, but he's bigger than any Lab or Chesapeake you ever saw and his muzzle's slimmer. He's a dull black with a narrow band of white across his upper chest."

For a moment Allan said nothing, but now he knew the origin of the slug he'd taken from Stormy's side. He tried to be very casual.

"Anybody own him?"

"If they did, they'd keep him home. He's an out and out tramp. You haven't seen him, eh?"

Allan said sarcastically, "Sure. He lives behind my woodpile and I have to beat him off with a club every time I want wood."

His hopes sank. Stormy a tramp, a homeless and unwanted wanderer in whom the hunting instinct was so powerful that he just had to hunt? Was it possible that he had turned against men? He'd neither stayed nor gone down when ordered to do so. Allan was grateful when Jeff changed the subject.

"How are you and the Torrances getting along?"

"As usual," Allan said shortly.

"Still fighting, huh?"

"I'm just leaving them alone."

"They leaving you alone, too?"

"So far."

Jeff grinned. "Things must be right sociable out your way."

Allan shrugged. "They could be better. Well, guess I'd better be going."

"How about another cup of coffee?"

"Next time, thanks."

Allan put on his jacket and cap, said goodbye to Jeff and his wife, went outside and left the boxed drake in Jeff's garage. Then he pulled his toboggan down the street to Johnny Malaming's store.

The store was a small building with a misleading MALAMING'S GREAT EMPORIUM spread in gilt letters across the front. But the inside was warm and comfortable, and fragrant with the odors of coffee, soap, tobacco, and the fresh pine boughs with which Johnny decorated his place of business.

Johnny himself, a little gnome of a man who had been in the Beaver Flowage since anyone could remember, came from the rear of the store.

"Hello, Johnny," Allan greeted him. "Cold enough to suit you?"

"You call this cold?" Johnny snorted. "You young'uns today are all sissies! Why many's the time, when I was a boy and my mother threw boilin' water out the door, it froze so fast we had hot ice!"

"The first time I heard that one," Allan said caustically, "I laughed so hard I almost kicked the bottom out of my cradle."

Johnny grinned. "What'll it be? The usual?"

Allan nodded and Johnny handed him four packs of Logger's Crimp Cut, Bill Marley's favorite pipe tobacco. Allan tucked them into his pocket and pulled out a piece of paper.

"Here's my grub list, Johnny. I'll pick it up on the way back."

Johnny took it and began to read, "A hundred pounds of flour, ten of bacon, hundred of dog meal—" He looked up questioningly. "When'd you get a dog?"

"Just lately."

"Hope it's a good'un. Say howdy to your dad and tell him I'll be up to see him first chance I get."

"Thanks, Johnny."

Allan walked down to the corner and waited. The bus that came along five minutes afterward stopped without any signal; Allan was on this corner every day visiting was permitted at Laceyville. The bus driver, a taciturn ex-logger, nodded amiably but didn't speak.

"Hi, Pete," Allan said. "Cold today."

"Yep."

There were only two other passengers, and Allan settled himself in an isolated seat while the bus rolled out of Tillotson and picked up speed on the ever-green-bordered road beyond. Thirty-two miles away was Laceyville Prison. Depending on whether one believed the authorities in charge or the inmates confined there, it was either the most modern of penal institutions or a veritable Siberia.

Allan stared unseeingly at the winterbound wilderness and did his best not to think. But he had to think, and presently his mind harked back to the mother he couldn't remember. He'd been a baby when she left Bill Marley and her infant son to cast her lot with a young engineer. There were as many versions of the story as there were gossips who cared to discuss it, but all sprang from only two basic beliefs. Some said that even his wife had finally become unable to bear Bill Marley's temper; others claimed that Bill had never had a temper until after Mary left.

The bus slowed. Allan made his way to the front and was ready when it stopped. A blast of frigid air rolled in when the door opened. Stepping down, Allan nodded at the driver.

"Be seeing you, Pete."

"Betcha."

The bus rumbled on as Allan made his way toward the grim stone building that was so grotesquely out of place in this setting. The guard at the gate nodded to the familiar visitor, admitted him without question, and Allan made his way to the visitors' room. The guard there, grown old in the penal service and mellowed rather than hardened by all it had taught him, greeted Allan cordially.

"Hello, young fellow."

"Good morning, sir."

"I'll have him here in a minute. Take a seat." The guard turned and spoke into a microphone.

Allan seated himself on the comfortable sofa, glad that at Laceyville only the most desperate inmates had to meet their visitors with a steel grill between them. He did his best to feel at ease. But despite pictures on the wall, the sofa, a writing table, carpeting, and other attempts to make this place one of informal cheer, a prison was still a prison and it never would be anything else. Then Bill Marley came in.

He was tall and sinewy, and his face bore the tales that had been written there by a thousand gales and storms and burning summer suns. But his eyes were haunted, and Allan felt a sudden great sympathy for the wild wing-tipped mallard that had exchanged limitless flyways for a little crate. Bill Marley had also been wild and free before he was cooped up. But now his eyes lighted as, for a moment, he forgot where he was. He could not go to the flyway, but with Allan, the flyway had come to him.

"Hello, Son!"

"Dad!"

They shook hands self-consciously, then went to the sofa and sat side by side.

"Well, duck season's over," his father said. "I've been keepin' count of the days. Did you have many hunters?"

"If I'd had one more," Allan evaded, "I don't know what I'd have done with him."

"I'm glad," his father said thankfully. "I'm glad you've kept it going, Son." His voice rose eagerly. "I'll bet Tom Morgan was there, and Martin Dele-hanty would never miss it. Ha! I remember when—"

He went on to speak of others, tried and tested hunters, many of whom had travelled long distances to hunt waterfowl with Bill Marley. Then his father asked about the flight. Omitting no detail, Allan told of the ducks and geese that had come in and the order in which they had arrived and departed.

"And now—" he said and hesitated.

"Yes?" Bill Marley was savoring each word as a starving person might another morsel of food.

About to speak of the dog, Allan decided not to. One outlaw in the Marley family was more than enough. If he knew about Stormy, Bill would worry.

"And now what?" his father asked.

"And now the lake is frozen," Allan amended hast-ily.

"Time's up," the guard said.

"One more question," Bill pressed. "Has—has there been any trouble with the Torrances?"

"No, Dad."

"Don't let there be any, Son! If they start any, avoid it any way you can. Run if you must, and never mind if they call you coward. Just don't have any trouble."

"I promise."

The haunted look was again in Bill Marley's eyes.

As though he'd forgotten all about them until now, Allan took the four packs of tobacco from his pocket.

"I brought these for you."

"Thank you, Son." Bill managed a smile. "And God bless you."

Soberly Allan awaited the next bus to Tillotson, rode it in, and walked over to Johnny Malaming's store. Johnny indicated the packed goods that had been on Allan's written order.

"There you are, Al. Everything's ready."

"Thanks, Johnny." Allan was immensely grateful because Johnny did not ask him how his father was. Being a man of the flyway himself, the storekeeper would know how Bill Marley was.

"Anything else?" Johnny asked.

"Just some information. Did you ever get around Cardsville much?"

"Sure. Used to buy baskets there for the summer trade."

"Ever run across any Zermeichs?"

"They're 'bout all you do run across. They're thicker'n Torrances this side of your lake."

"Do you know a Jacob Zermeich?"

"Yup, and if he bit himself he'd die of his own poison. Meanest man I ever knew. I saw him take a chain to a horse once; it's the one time in my life I'd have killed a man if I had a gun. Jake mistreats every critter on his place. Say, what's this all about?"

"Well, jobs are hard to get here," Allan said vaguely, "and next spring, if I went to Cardsville . . ."

"Sure, sure," Johnny answered sympathetically. "But don't work for old Jake Zermeich!"

"I won't, and thanks for the information. So long."

Allan had learned what he wanted to know. If you misused Stormy, he'd strike back. Beyond any doubt that's why he was now a reputed man killer.

3. First Expedition

Because the deep drifts were already broken, it was not as hard to pull the loaded toboggan back as it had been to break a trail out. The wind had dropped, and the temperature had risen to about zero. This left the snow crisp enough for the toboggan to glide smoothly while at the same time the weather seemed relatively mild. As he crossed the Joe Torrance farm, Allan devoted himself to serious thought.

He was positive now that Stormy had attacked Jacob Zermeich only because he was being badly mistreated. Now that the dog was an outlaw, nobody else would want him. He hadn't responded to commands, true, but Allan put that down to distrust. And he was a magnificent hunter as proved by the fact that the drake he'd put in Allan's hand hadn't had so much as one ruffled feather. Despite his dubious reputation, Stormy was the dog Allan had been looking for all his life.

But when he saw Joe Torrance going from his barn to his house, the very real obstacles in the path of adopting the big mongrel, or of just keeping him alive, were brought forcibly home. Reputedly Stormy was an outlaw, a beast that had turned against man, and thus men must turn against him. Should he be sighted, he would be summarily killed. If Allan thought he was really a man killer, he himself would do away with the dog. But he didn't think so.

Stormy's retrieving the wing-tipped drake had nothing whatever to do with his attitude toward human beings. However, after Allan took him into the house, he had shown not the faintest sign of hostility. True, he had not shown any friendliness either, but his reserve and aloof manner might easily be explained by the fact that he had suffered abuse.

Allan had a momentary wild hope that Stormy's presence on his place would be natural cause for assumption that he had either bought the dog or someone had given it to him. The fallacy of such wishful thinking became apparent almost at once. Stormy was so big that his size alone marked him, and practically everyone must have seen the picture in the paper.

Allan looked at the Torrance house and grimaced. It had been the elder Marley and Torrance who'd fought, but the youngsters had inherited the bitterness of that quarrel. Even though they were leaving each other alone, the feud still smoldered. If Joe Torrance knew Allan was keeping an outlaw dog, he'd drop anything to go into Tillotson and spread the news. Allan admitted honestly that, if he found any way to make trouble for Joe Torrance, he'd probably do it too.

Still, maybe he could keep anyone from seeing this dog. The Marley property extended all the way around the lake and for a considerable distance back from the shores, and all of it was wooded. Almost never were there visitors; few people cared to walk to this lake when hunting and fishing as good were more accessible elsewhere. If he could just keep Stormy on his own place, and never let anyone see him, people would forget about the outlaw dog in time, and the problem would be solved. It seemed a rather uncertain solution, but at the moment it was the only one that presented itself.

By the time he reached the lake ice, the wind had increased again. Allan ducked his chin into the wool collar of his coat and bent his head, while he fought to keep the wind from making the toboggan sideslip. Zero cold was not unbearable or even uncomfortable, but zero cold with a high wind was something entirely different. The Beaver Flowage had had an early winter which evidently was also going to be a cold one. It had happened that way the year before, and usually two or three severe winters followed each other.

Allan swerved from the lake toward the house, and despite the cold found himself sweating as he fought his toboggan through drifts that the wind had again piled up. He pulled it as close to the porch as he could and went in to get warm. He found the fire low, and a thin shell of ice forming on the water pails. Stormy rose and stretched when Allan entered but did not come to meet him. Allan looked keenly at the dog.

As far as he was able to see, there was no suggestion of the killer in the brown eyes. Instead, there was the same untamed quality that Allan had noticed before, something that seemed to share in part with the cry of the wild goose, the flashing wings of a flying teal, the lake when an angry wind churned it into whitecaps, the brooding trees, and the forest earth itself. This dog was no artificial creature shaped by selective breeding to do a certain task for man or fill a prescribed niche. He was elemental as the flyway itself, and as natural. It was a quality with which Allan had been born, and one he understood thoroughly.

Stormy stood on three legs, lifting the right foot, as Allan went forward to poke up the ashes in the stove and throw in fresh wood. Despite the bullet wound the dog did not waver on those three feet; he had good recuperative powers. A 30-30 slug where Stormy had taken it would not have killed him unless it had mushroomed. But how many dogs would have travelled far with such a wound? Stormy must have come at least twenty miles after being shot, and had still retrieved a duck from icy water. Allan grinned.

"Tough guy, eh? Well, wait'll I get warm, Stormy."

His voice held none of that affectionate condescension with which most people address dogs, but a conversational liking and respect. At various times he had heard people assert that dogs are better than humans, and thought such arguments silly. Dogs were not humans, nor humans dogs, and there was no sane basis for comparing the two. But as an animal, a fellow mortal, Allan could not help sensing and admiring the superiority of this great beast. Stormy had no pedigree, but he was as sure of himself as any thoroughbred.

When Allan went outside to start bringing in his supplies, Stormy limped beside him. There was no more blood trickling from the wound, but he'd left a stain on the floor where he had been lying. Allan's worry about the dog's safety began afresh. The very fact that Stormy had been at Cardsville, and then had unexpectedly shown up here, fifty miles away, was evidence that he was a wanderer. It was highly probable that he would go wandering again when the mood struck him. If he did, and were seen, the next rifleman might not merely wound him.

As Allan shouldered the hundred-pound sack of flour he stole a sidewise glance at Stormy, who was unconcernedly facing the cold breeze that swept in from the lake. Allan thought of a stout chain, and immediately dismissed the idea. A chain would keep Stormy from roving, but it wouldn't make him any man's dog. The bullet wound, that must hurt, might prove a blessing in disguise insofar as it might keep the dog from going elsewhere until something happened to cement relations between them and cause the big mongrel to stay with Allan of his own free will. No other way would ever work.

When the last of his supplies were carried in, Allan pulled his toboggan around to the rear. Stormy walked beside him, and stood gravely as Allan lifted the toboggan onto its rack. Coming around to the front again, they both stopped and looked out across the lake.   ·

Primarily this was flyway country, a vast highway for hordes of waterfowl that thronged down it in autumn and up it in spring. But it was also fishing country; Allan knew that, beneath the ice right now, mighty-jawed pike were on the prowl for bluegills, perch, and shiners. There were bass too, and last summer a colony of beaver had moved in, so that the winter-time lake became a world all its own.

Across the lake and to the north, the direction in which Allan was looking, was a mingled evergreen-hardwood forest that stretched for a hundred miles that he knew of. It was a strange land, with here and there a patch of high, fertile land suitable for farming. But mostly there were lakes without number, and ponds too small to be dignified with the name of lake. There were extensive areas that had the outward aspect of firm earth, but that actually were mere shells of earth floating on water. They quivered like jelly when one walked across them, and almost anywhere, in such places, it was possible to poke a hole through the shell and catch fish. Except in winter, when they were frozen hard, such areas could be highly dangerous.

The forest, too, presented its own never-ending drama of life and death. Cottontail rabbits, huddled in their sets, became the coveted prizes of hungry foxes and coyotes. Big-footed snowshoe hares might or might not see the lynx ambushed along their runways. Safe in some copse or cavern, bears slept the winter away. Furtive deer slunk through the thickets, and great gray timber wolves came to hunt them. Sinewy marten chased terrified squirrels on spectacular aerial routes that involved wild leaps from branch to branch and tree to tree. Plodding wolverenes, for the mere sake of destruction, often rended or defiled whatever they did not care to eat.

As Allan watched, a doe came out of the darkening

woods, stepped lightly down to the lake, and stopped just short of the ice. She was grayish-brown, the deer's winter color, but in the lowering twilight and against the pure white background, she presented a jet-black silhouette. In the doe Allan saw a summation of everything represented by the lake, the forest, the flyway, and the life he and his father had led until a year ago. He had to keep things going, somehow. Allan spent as sparingly as possible, and took as much of his livelihood as he could from the lake and the country around it. But try as he would, his principal source of cash income, the trapping of furs, did not replace the money he must use for groceries and other necessities. He could do well enough if only the waterfowl hunters would come back, but apparently they wouldn't if they had to walk.

He turned moodily to the dog. "Coming in, Stormy?"

They entered the house together, and the now-glowing stove sent welcome waves of heat across the room. Stormy curled up beside the wall away from the stove, while Allan filled the teakettle. He poured a generous portion of dog meal into a dish, mixed it with warm water from the kettle, and fed Stormy. The big mongrel ate with quiet dignity, and returned to his bed. Allan set about preparing his own supper of pork chops, potatoes, canned carrots, and coffee.

As he turned the browning pork chops with a fork, Allan calculated in his mind the sum he had spent that day, the amount left, what he could expect to earn on his trapline this winter. He could make out all right until his father was released. But what would happen when Bill Marley came back from Laceyville and found that the Torrances had effectively cut off their duck-hunting business?

Stormy rose, padded to the door, and stood expectantly before it. After some hesitation, Allan let him out. As he did, he felt suddenly downhearted. Vivid in his memory was the picture of this dog, with a 30-30 slug in his side, retrieving the wing-tipped drake because he just had to hunt. Stormy might be called an outlaw, but luck had come to Allan's lake with him and luck would go when he left.

Then, an hour later, Stormy woofed softly at the door and Allan rose happily to let him in. The big dog hadn't wanted to run away, but merely to ramble outside for a while. Allan stood in the doorway a moment, and knew from the changing wind and rising temperature that tomorrow probably would bring more snow. Snow or not, he had to go out on his traplines.

Stormy stretched out along the far wall. Allan blew out the oil lamp, went to bed, and thought it was only a few minutes until he awakened to a dark morning. He lay drowsily in bed, aware of the great quiet that held sway outside. Seemingly there was not a puff of wind; last night's forecast of snow was going to be fulfilled.

Allan swung out of bed and lighted the lamp. Without making any move to approach, Stormy rose to his feet and watched him. Allan poked the gray ashes in his stove, threw kindling on, and prepared another bowl of meal for Stormy. Yesterday a hundred pounds of dog meal had seemed a lot, all any one animal could be expected to consume for a considerable length of time. But he realized that besides being very big, Stormy had had little to eat. Allan fed the dog, mixed a bowl of flapjack batter for himself, and debated what to do as he dropped the pancakes onto a greased griddle.

He had bobcat, coyote, fox, and mink traps set in the forest bogland to the north. Should he risk taking Stormy with him? If the dog were well he wouldn't hesitate, but Stormy had been hurt. However, it was necessary to make only about a four-mile swing today and the wound did not seem to bother the dog unduly. Without making up his mind one way or the other, Allan sat down to eat. Finished, he washed the dishes and stepped outside.

Thin gray dawn was creeping out of a cloud-laden sky into a breathless world. It was so warm that, despite his lack of a jacket, Allan did not feel cold. There was no wind at all, and the weather signs, familiar throughout Allan's whole life, told him to expect snow shortly. However, out in the forest it would not drift nearly as much as it had yesterday on the comparatively treeless open country he had crossed. Stormy should have little trouble if they took it slowly enough, and they could always return if he did find it difficult going. Since Allan wanted to win the big dog over, there was no time like the present to begin.

Allan went back inside to assemble his kit, including a .22 revolver and a hatchet that were slung in sheaths on opposite sides of his belt. For a pocket knife, he preferred a complex thing with three cutting blades, an awl, screw-driver, can opener, and pair of scissors, that was practically a small tool chest within itself. He carried no pack basket. Since animals almost invariably froze before he could get them home and must be thawed again before they could be skinned, he liked to pelt his catch where he took it; pelts were easy to carry. He made two sandwiches which he wrapped first in wax paper, then in newspaper and thrust them in the spacious rear pocket of his hunting jacket. Finally he buttoned in an inside pocket that indispensable accessory, a watertight tube of matches. Ready, he put his wool cap on, slung his snowshoes over his shoulder, and with Stormy beside him, struck straight across the lake ice.

The weather was almost uncomfortably warm, so Allan left his jacket unbuttoned and pushed his cap back on his head. But the frigid cold of yesterday had frozen the ice so hard that a truck might have crossed it safely. As the day lightened, the sea of clouds that surged across the sky promised snow to come. But there was no indication of a severe storm.

Stormy walked to his right, staying about three feet away, and though he still limped, there was no evidence that his wound was bothering him. Then they were across the lake and at the border of the forest.

Balsam Creek, a stream whose sources were a thousand hidden springs and seepages, emptied into the lake at this point. During the fall rains the stream always flooded over both banks. An early cold spell, such as this year's, froze it at the high-water mark.

Then when the water receded to normal levels, in places there might be three feet of air between the surface of Balsam Creek and the bottom of the ice. Consequently, the creek was now a maze of ice canyons and runways.

Mink prowling the lake shore invariably went up Balsam Creek under an overhanging ledge of rock which, because it could never be reached by snow or ice to bury a trap or freeze it, made a perfect blind set. Allan had put a trap there, but it must have had a defective link, for all that remained were the ring and the flexible wire with which it had been fastened. Plainly imprinted in snow just beyond the ledge were tracks of a mink with a trap on its foot. The tracks led into a narrow fissure beneath the ice.

Allan muttered to himself. It was bad to lose a valuable mink pelt, but it was far worse to imagine a mink with a trap on its foot suffering a lingering death beneath the ice. Of course there was a possibility that it had fallen into the water, and if so it would surely drown with the weight of the trap pulling it down. But there was also a possibility that it hadn't drowned; mink are unbelievably vital. It would take one a long time to starve to death and the trap alone would never kill it.

Allan noticed suddenly that Stormy was no longer at his side, but had gone about twenty feet up the ice of Balsam Creek and was snuffling intently into a fissure there. Allan looked at him in surprise. He'd seen Stormy retrieve the duck, but there was no reason to suppose that he would also hunt a mink. However, Stormy was a mongrel, a mixture of breeds, and a rare few of such dogs are inclined to a mixture of activities. When one was, it was apt to be a remarkable dog indeed.

Allan walked up beside Stormy, dropped to his hands and knees, put his nose to the same fissure the dog was snuffling, and very faintly but surely smelled the strong musk that is the distinctive trail mark of an enraged, aroused, or frightened mink. Stormy was certainly hunting the mink. If he'd continue to do so, there was a distinct possibility that they'd find it.

"All right, Stormy!" Allan said encouragingly. "Let's get him!"

The retriever walked slowly up the ice, swerved to sniff at a fissure on the far side, crossed to one on the near, and made a thorough investigation of a crack in the center. Allan watched, perplexed. This aimless wandering and snuffling couldn't mean anything. Then suddenly he knew. The mink's scent couldn't possibly penetrate through the ice, but only through cracks and fissures. In investigating every one of them, Stormy was using his head as well as his nose. Allan dropped behind and let the dog work.

Progress was necessarily slow, for there were stretches of Balsam Creek that might have a hundred openings, which varied from tiny cracks and holes to fissures into which Stormy could lower his entire head. But it was fascinating, and Allan forgot the passage of time as he watched Stormy work out the path the mink had taken. Finally the big dog came to a halt over a two-inch crack. Dropping beside him, Allan saw an exhausted mink on a ledge a couple of feet below. The trap had finally snagged, and the animal could go no farther.

Allan drew his revolver, took careful aim, shot, and the mink went limp. Allan used his hatchet to widen the crack, and finally took a fine dark mink from the ledge.

When he arose, he was aware of what he would have noticed long ago had he not been so interested in watching Stormy trail the mink. The wind had freshened, the clouds had gathered and lowered as though they meant to smother the earth. Snow was whirling thickly, and though Allan's watch told him that it was not yet mid-day, there was an almost weird sense of nightfall.

"Come on, Stormy!" he said commandingly.

Making sure the dog was at his side, he turned and ran for the forest.

4. Stormbound

As Allan ran across the ice toward the forest, he fought the panic that rose within him. The tree line, that should have been starkly clear against the snowy background, was almost obscured. He saw it not as a forest whose separate trees were distinct, but as a blurred whole that at times almost disappeared behind swirling drapes of snow.

The storm seemed to have burst upon him silently and with no warning whatever, but he knew that was an illusion. He was to blame for being caught, for had he not been so intent on watching Stormy trail the mink he would have realized that a storm was about to break while he still had time to return to his house. Now it was too late to return. The storm was gathering fury by the second, and if it caught him out on the ice he would be unable to see a single landmark; he might walk in a circle until exhausted. His only hope lay in the forest, where he could wait the storm out under some sort of shelter. He'd camped out before in winter and been not only safe but comfortable. This was different only because of the storm, he told himself.

Stormy beside him, Allan left the ice and plunged into knee-deep snow. He forced a way through the willows that lined the banks of Balsam Creek, and ducked into a grove of bushy hemlocks, which broke the strength of the snow-driving wind. Looking about and wondering what to do next, he noticed the dog.

A shadow in the semi-gloom, Stormy was sitting on his haunches a little to one side and looking steadily at Allan. Unaccountably Allan thought of a picture he had seen in some thriller magazine. It was a black leopard at twilight, and its body blended so well with the darkness that it seemed part of it. Its glaring, yellow eyes were fixed on something as it deliberated the next move.

Allan felt uncomfortable. There was no threat in the dog's attitude, but Stormy was intent in the same way, and Allan could not rid himself of a feeling that the dog was studying him. They were facing a crisis, one not without danger, and Allan sensed that the dog was deliberately waiting to see what he would do next.

Wrenching his eyes from Stormy, Allan slipped the snowshoes from his shoulder, stuck one upright in the snow, and started digging with the other. He worked fast, using the snow he removed to build a wall on all four sides. At the same time he was cautious. His digging might uncover a dead snag or stump upon which the snowshoe could be broken. He found no such obstacle, and when the toe of his snowshoe brushed cushiony hemlock needles he widened the hole already dug into a pit about four feet square. He glanced quickly at Stormy, and away again.

A week from now he'd remember, and doubtless

smile about, the time a dog sat in judgment to see how he would react to a dangerous predicament. But at the moment he could not rid himself of the notion that Stormy was really studying him and did want to know what he would do. Suddenly he felt a warm bond between himself and the big mongrel. In their way both were outcasts, and both had to meet special problems because of it. Well, he'd better do something about this one.

He leaned his snowshoes against the side of the pit, broke a trail through the snow to the nearest hemlock, and stooped to run his hands up and down its lower trunk. Such small, closely growing evergreens always had dead twigs on the bottom. As Allan found them he broke them off and wrapped them in his jacket, which he laid in the snow. Then he plunged farther into deep snow for more wood.

He did not want to cut any of those trees immediately adjoining his pit for they would help soften the wind and turn the snow, but presently he found one he could take. Allan was about to cut it with his belt hatchet when he saw a small, dead tree so close that its brittle branches intertwined with the green of the living hemlock. Bracing his back against the green one, and helping maintain a balance by thrusting his left leg into the snow, Allan placed his right foot against the dead tree and rocked it forward. He let it swing back and rocked again, increasing the tempo and each time shoving the dead tree farther. After a moment, it snapped and tumbled in the snow.

Allan dragged the dead tree back to the pit and used the blunt end of his hatchet to smash the brittle branches from the parent trunk. Then he chopped an eighteen-inch length from the trunk itself and, laying an end of the remainder on it, broke the rest of the trunk into suitable lengths by jumping on it.

He went back for his jacket, laid the twigs it had protected in the bottom of his pit, and slipped into the jacket. Going to his knees, he removed the outer layer of paper from his sandwiches, and upon it arranged dead twigs no bigger than match sticks. Carefully he added larger pieces of wood. Then, unbuttoning his jacket and holding the left side out to form a windbreak, he struck a match and applied it to the paper. The paper flared. Flame crackled through the twigs and ate its way into the larger pieces of wood. Allan added the rest of his dead tree, and the leaping fire burned a bright hole in the semi-gloom.

Following the path he'd already broken, and which was already partly snow-filled, Allan returned to where he'd cut the dead tree and looked back. The fire was plainly seen. Looking back every few steps, Allan plowed through the snow until, when he looked over his shoulder, the fire was only a dull glow through sheets of swirling snow. Allan cut another tree, dragged it back to his pit, broke it up, and went out again.

With the fire as a hub, his wood-gathering excursions became the spokes of a wheel. Never travelling out of sight of the fire, but always going far enough so that it was only dimly seen to cover as large an area as possible, he cut trees and dragged them back. Allan took all the dead trees he found, but green wood as well because it burned longer. He cut or smashed the branches off with his hatchet and used the green ones to carpet the floor of his pit. The trunks he stood against the snow wall that surrounded him, for future use.

The storm was now reaching its peak, and all about, snow whirled furiously down. Busy gathering enough wood to last, Allan had paid no attention to the time, but he thought that most of the day was gone. However, when he tilted his watch beside the fire so that he could see the dial, he discovered that it was only half-past three.

Allan settled himself by the fire and took stock of his situation. Rarely did such storms last longer than twenty-four hours. But every now and again they raged for periods of three days to a week. Should this be such a storm, Allan knew that he was in for serious trouble. He had wood and shelter, but no food except the two sandwiches.

For all that he was calm, almost serene. This was what life was like in the Beaver Flowage. It was a wild, raw, and sometimes dangerous land, but even in this crisis Allan loved it. There was something elemental here. It had nothing to do with lives so well-ordered that those who lived them always knew exactly what they would be doing on any given day. It was a country for the wild ducks and geese, the deer, the fish beneath the ice, the dog across the fire, and the sportsmen who came every year to fish or hunt. As he sat beside his fire, Allan knew that the fish sportsmen caught and the waterfowl they bagged were only part of the lure that drew them. They came also because they were weary of conformity and easy living. Allan understood completely, because he himself could never leave the Beaver Flowage. Born to the elemental, he could not live without it.

He skinned the mink by the fire's light, thrust the limp pelt into his jacket, and speculatively regarded the carcass. Then he grimaced and threw it out in the snow. At best it was a few ounces of meat permeated with foul musk. Even Stormy wouldn't want it. A moment later he climbed out of the pit, thrust his hand into the snow where the mink carcass had landed, and recovered it. This was a time for thinking, and in lightly throwing the carcass away, he had not thought. Seating himself again, he looked at the dog lying across the fire.

Stormy was lying down with his head on his paws and his unblinking eyes fixed on the fire. Allan's fleeting smile was warm. Almost any other dog would have been crowding anxiously near and looking to his master for reassurance. Stormy was meeting the situation like a wolf, and making the best of it. He had no intention of looking to anything or anybody except himself. Allan had the feeling that Stormy could never be bent or beaten into any conventional mold. But he also thought that, if he should ever be fortunate enough to win the big dog's allegiance, he would win all of it.

Turning his mind back to their stormbound plight, Allan took the knife from his pocket, opened the pliers that folded into the handle, and snipped the chain from the trap in which he had taken the mink. He snipped again, so that the end link formed a hook.

Closing the pliers and opening the file blade, he filed a needle point on the hook. Then, removing his leather belt, he sliced thin strips from either side and tied them together to form one six-foot length. He tested it for strength by snapping it between his fingers, and when the leather thong did not break he tied one end securely to the trap chain.

Next he took his pacs off, stripped off the outer of the two pairs of wool socks he wore and again bent to work by the fire's light. He opened the awl blade of his knife, pricked a sock, and carefully began to unravel it. It was slow and tedious work, but he was going nowhere for a while; there was plenty of time.

Allan tied the strands of yarn together, rolled them into a ball, and began on the other sock. He tied those strands to the first, and when he was finished thrust the ball of yarn into his pocket. He had a plan. If it did not work, nothing was lost. If it did, no matter how long the storm lasted, he and Stormy would see it through. But night had fallen in earnest now. He could do nothing except wait for morning.

Allan took the sandwiches from his pocket, removed one, and put the other back. He cut the one in half.

"Chow time, Stormy," he announced, holding out one half.

The big dog rose, came around the fire, accepted and ate his half of the sandwich, and went back to lie in his original bed. While Allan chewed his share of the sandwich he concentrated on the dancing flames.

Only a fool would deliberately invite a predicament such as this, but now that he was in it, Allan found it not all bad. Petty worries were far away and insignificant. The world consisted of himself, his dog, the fire, and the storm that kept them prisoners. But being a prisoner of a storm was quite different from being a captive of men. Allan thought of his father, who had been caught by the elements many times. How he would prefer this to his cell at Laceyville!

Presently he leaned his head on his upraised knees and dozed until he was awakened by cold. The fire had subsided to a mass of glowing coals that somehow seemed to defy the storm. Allan rose, added wood to his fire, and on sudden impulse divided the remaining sandwich with Stormy. Now he had no food at all, but remained unworried. He sat down to doze until cold should again awaken him.

Morning came, but rather than a brightening of the day, it was more a lessening of the night. Wind-driven snow continued to fall so fast that only those trees within twenty-five feet or less were visible. The snowbank Allan had erected around his pit was covered with ten inches of new fall, beautiful but sinister.

Stormy rose, rid his black fur of snow with a single vigorous shake of his body, and waited expectantly. Allan got up and stretched, ready to carry out his plan formed during the night.

Storms such as this always came from the northwest. It followed, therefore, that Balsam Creek lay southeast, or with the wind. Allan built his fire so high that leaping flames began to melt the surrounding snowbank. Satisfied that it would last, he put a foot-long piece of wood in the game pocket of his jacket, laced his snowshoes on, caught up the mink carcass, and with Stormy following in the path he broke, started toward the creek.

Every few steps he looked back over his shoulder. When he was thirty feet from the fire, which he still saw plainly, he tied one end of the ball of yarn to a tree and continued, unrolling the ball as he did so. He travelled slowly, for the yarn was fragile and he dared not risk breaking it. Presently the tips of the willows bordering Balsam Creek bent beneath his snowshoes and then he was on the creek itself.

Allan anchored the end of his yarn with the chunk of wood he'd brought along, unlaced his snowshoes, and laid the piece of wood on one of them. With the other, he methodically began to dig through the snow. He did not hurry, or even attempt to lift any heavy weight of snow, for his very life depended on the snowshoes and he dared not break them. Reaching ice, he widened the hole so that it was big enough for him to move about.

Taking the hatchet from his sheath, he knelt and scarred the ice, averting his face as a stinging shower of ice pellets struck him. Stormy looked interestedly on as Allan continued to chop. Twenty minutes later he removed a square foot of ice eight inches thick, and the slow water of Balsam Creek rose part way into the hole. Allan lay prone to look into the creek.

The day was half dark and half light, but he could see the creek's sandy bottom for the water at this place was only two or three feet deep. After a moment a school of shiners darted past. Then he saw a thin film of silt that could have been caused only by some disturbance upstream, and crossed his fingers. All the signs looked hopeful.

Taking the chain and thong from his pocket, Allan strung a piece of the mink's red carcass on his improvised hook and lowered it through the hole. He wrapped the thong loosely about his wrist and sat quietly. It was a calculated rather than a fretful waiting. There were times to hurry, but there were also times when haste defeated the objective.

About ten minutes later, as though of its own volition, the leather thong began to slide into the water. Allan let it go, knowing that he had read the signs correctly. Small fish had sought a haven in these shallow waters. Big pike, hungry most of the time and ravenous in winter, were hunting them. A pike had taken Allan's bait, and now everything must be done exactly right. The chain and thong would hold even a big fish, but at best the hook was makeshift. For one thing it was too small, and for another it had no barb. Almost the only chance of landing a fish lay in letting whatever had the bait swallow it before setting the hook.

Allan let the thong play out to the last possible inch, then jerked it. Instant resistance told him that he had his quarry, but it was still possible to pull the hook out if he was not careful or if he used too much strength. Allan merely held on, took up the slack when there was any, and let the fish tire itself in a series of savage rushes. Then, inch by inch, he shortened the thong and worked his catch up to the hole he'd chopped in the ice. Fifteen minutes after he'd set the hook, he lifted a big pike through the hole.

For a moment he sat enthralled, too happy even to move. It seemed a long while ago that the storm had broken and he had run for shelter; almost it seemed like another person. Now he knew that, no matter what happened, he would never again be afraid of weather. He had won because he had refused to lose.

"We'll eat now, Stormy," he told the dog.

Putting on his snowshoes and swinging the pike over his shoulder, Allan picked up the stick to which his yarn was attached, and followed the strands back to where he could see the fire. The snow still whirled and the wind still blew, but now there was no threat in either. The storm was merely something to be waited out until he could return home.

He half slid and half stepped into his pit, built up the fire, and cleaned and beheaded the pike. The offal he saved; cannibal pike would bite on it as readily as they would on anything else, if he needed to go fishing again. Allan sliced his fish down the back and stripped the firm white flesh away from the backbone.

Unexpectedly, Stormy rose and walked around the fire. He nudged Allan's thigh with his shoulder, and flicked his tongue out to brush the youth's cheek. When Allan ruffled his ears, the big dog's tail wagged happily; Stormy had finally chosen his master.

That night the storm abated.

5. Stormy's Training

Still a little way out on the snow-covered lake, Allan stopped and looked at his house. The winterbound oaks, maples, and birches that bordered the lake stood black and cold against the drifted snow. The heavily needled pines and hemlocks, whose branches caught the snow instead of letting it fall through, had only an occasional green branch showing in a natural position. All the rest drooped earthward, borne down by the weight of the snow clinging to them.

The northwest side of the Marley house, the wing containing the bunks and lockers, was drifted to the gabled roof and both windows wore a curtain of snow. That was good rather than bad; such a drift acted as natural insulation to help keep the house warm. The closed windows would make no difference, for Allan never used the bunk room anyway. But the fact that the porch was also drifted full meant that he couldn't even get in until he shovelled it free. He groaned in mock dismay.

When Allan swung to look back over his trail, Stormy wagged his tail amiably. Allan looked fondly at the big dog. He still liked to fancy that Stormy really had had him under critical observation, and had decided that he was a worthy master because of the way Allan had faced danger. One thing Allan knew for sure; the second night out, with Stormy sleeping across his feet and helping him keep warm, had been a lot more comfortable than the first.

Allan looked at his snowshoe tracks, the only break in the virgin snow that covered the ice. They were deep, all right. In ordinary winters he started breaking his trapline trails with the first four-inch snowfall. As new snow fell he packed it down, so that on clear days there was always a hard trail and often he could leave his snowshoes home. But this was no ordinary winter. He'd fought deep snow all the way from the hemlocks, and it had taken him almost three hours to come two and a quarter miles. True, part of that time was accounted for because he'd had to stop and wait for Stormy. Trailing in Allan's snowshoe tracks, the big dog frequently broke through and had to scramble and paw his way back to packed snow.

Allan ruffled Stormy's ears with his mittened hand.

"Come on," Allan told him. "It doesn't look as though any good fairy's going to open that door for us, dog, so I reckon we'll have to do it ourselves. Or at least I will."

He made his way to a tool shed behind the house. Allan's grandfather, who'd built both house and shed, had obviously observed prevailing winter winds before erecting the latter structure and planned accordingly. The shed's door was on the south side and the building itself had created a vacuum on that side as the wind roared around it. There was a five-foot drift two yards from the door, but almost no snow between the drift and the shed. Allan got a shovel and snowshoed back to the porch.

There had been no thaw and subsequent freeze to form a crust, but the wind had driven this snow so furiously that it was tight-packed. Allan cut it with the end of his shovel and lifted it out in squares. As he cut and lifted them he piled the snow blocks on the northwest side. Should there be another such storm, the pile of snow would help prevent the porch's drifting full a second time.

As soon as a space was cleared in front of the porch, Allan removed his snowshoes and thrust them upright in the snow. Stormy, who'd been fighting the snow while still weakened from the bullet wound, sat on his haunches with his tail curled around his rear, and watched contentedly as Allan continued to work. Allan raised the shovel shoulder high to attack drifted snow on the porch. In an hour the door was free, and Allan went in, Stormy padding behind him.

Long ago, Allan's father had taught him the importance of a full woodbox and as usual he had filled it before leaving. Now Allan laid shavings in his heating stove, arranged kindling on top of the shavings, and lighted his fire. When the kindling blazed, he added chunk wood and adjusted the dampers. Catching up his biggest coffee pot, he stepped outside, packed it full of snow and put it on top of the heating stove. He stripped the label from a can of pork and beans and dropped the can into the warming water to heat.

No longer aloof but seemingly intrigued by everything Allan did, Stormy watched him closely, tail thumping from time to time. The serenity Allan had found while he crouched beside his fire and let the storm rage was still with him, and his worries seemed small indeed. No longer was he alone, and with Stormy beside him nothing seemed hopeless or impossible.

When the water in the coffee pot began to bubble, Allan took his can of pork and beans out with a pair of pliers, punched a hole in the can to let the steam escape, and dumped a handful of coffee into the pot. While he waited for the coffee to brew, he mixed a dish of meal for Stormy. Then he opened the beans, poured strong, scalding coffee into a thick mug, and sat down to his meal.

He ate the pork and beans directly from the can, gulped the black coffee, and thought he had never tasted anything so delicious. Unsalted fish broiled over an open fire while a storm raged was probably very romantic. But civilized food had such fare beat by a country mile, even though he was eating it in a rather uncivilized manner. Allan finished the pork and beans, drank two more cups of coffee, and felt ready to go to work again.

There was much to do, and foremost among the tasks at hand was clearing the windows. Oil for his lamps cost money and he could not afford to be prodigal. Though the winter days were short, and most of them were far from bright, such daylight as there was should be utilized.

Allan shovelled the rest of the snow from his porch, cleared a path to his wood and tool sheds, and finally started shoveling toward his fur shed. When he reached the latter, he started to shake away the snow that had collected over the hasp, and muttered sharply when the hasp came away in his hand.

Anger rose like a burning flame. Somebody, probably a Torrance, had broken in. Allan yanked the door open to discover that the seven weasel pelts that he'd taken and stored for bounty were no longer there. He turned toward the house, but halted after three steps. The Marleys already had more trouble than they needed and the seven weasel pelts represented no great value anyhow. It was better to forget them than to start another quarrel. Fortunately there had been nothing really valuable in the fur shed. But how about . . . ?

On sudden impulse Allan ran to the house, pulled back the loose floor board beneath which he and his father had kept their little hoard of money, and lifted out the tin box. It had not been disturbed; the money was intact.

Returning to the fur shed, Allan pulled the lustrous mink pelt over a stretching board. He stretched it fur side in, so that the pelt would dry properly, and carefully felt the silky tail to make sure all the bone was out. Some trappers considered these minor details, but by skinning, stretching, and fleshing his pelts properly, and trapping only when furs were prime, Allan always received premium prices for his catch.

By the time he had finished and refilled the woodbox, night had come again. Allan prepared and ate his evening meal, washed the dishes, then turned happily to Stormy. There was more work to be done.

This was what he'd been waiting for ever since he'd decided to his own satisfaction that as far as obedience was concerned Stormy had given allegiance only to old Del Crossman. The dog must learn to obey Allan if he was ever to become the retriever of Allan's dreams, and the gentle way was the only one. Even if Allan considered such a course proper, it would be futile and perhaps disastrous to try teaching by force. Jacob Zermeich had found that out.

Sitting well away from the stove, for he did not like much heat, Stormy followed with his eyes as Allan walked halfway across the floor. Allan knelt, snapped his fingers, and said quietly, "Come here, Stormy."

Immediately the big mongrel rose, padded to Allan, and waited expectantly. Allan let his left hand ruffle Stormy's ears, and after a moment his right stole to the big mongrel's haunches. Stormy turned to see what he was doing, then looked back at Allan's face.

"Sit," Allan said quietly.

At the same time he exerted gentle pressure with his right hand. Stormy's rear stiffened; his muscles tensed. Allan knew that he couldn't make the dog sit if he did not feel like it; he was far too big and powerful to be forced. Although he didn't obey, his eyes remained questioning. Stormy did not resent what was being done; he just wanted to know why it should be done.

Allan tried again, and again met resistance. But on the fourth attempt, as though he suddenly understood what was wanted, Stormy settled slowly back on his haunches. Allan praised him with words and caresses.

"Good boy! That's it Stormy! Good boy!"

Stormy's eyes gleamed. His tongue lolled slightly and his jaws seemed to frame a happy grin. His tail wagged. As Allan had thought, when he finally gave himself he did so completely. Though he would never be servile he did want to please, and he'd do whatever Allan wished as long as he understood what that was. After a moment Allan took his hand from the dog's rear quarters.

"All right," he said.

Stormy rose, not because he understood the command but because he wanted to get up anyway. His tail continued to wag as he sniffed Allan's hand, and he tagged behind as Allan paced across the floor.

After a couple of minutes Allan repeated, "Sit."

Stormy touched his rear to the floor and immediately bounced up. Kneeling, his left hand stroking the dog's ears and his right pressing down on Stormy's hind quarters, Allan again gave the command to sit and held Stormy until the "all right" order.

Twenty minutes later Stormy would sit on command and stay until told he might get up. Allan's happiness mounted. He'd seen many intelligent dogs, for intelligence was a basic requisite for any good retriever. But never before had he known of a dog's learning so quickly. However, one lesson was enough for one night. Allan went to bed and Stormy curled up in his favorite place against the wall farthest from the fire.

The next morning the weather was clear and Allan dressed for the trail. He had traps out and must cover them; he could afford to overlook no opportunity to earn another dollar. Not limping now and showing no trace of weariness, Stormy crowded out the door with him and followed Allan to the tool shed.

Allan exchanged the gloves he wore for a pair that dangled from a hook. Careful to touch nothing except with these gloves, he loaded a pack basket with a small shovel, a roll of flexible wire, two number one-and-a-half and two number two traps, a strip of canvas, an old hatchet, and a roll of tissue. Finally, with a grimace, he picked up a four-ounce capped bottle. This contained fox scent and was composed of fish oil, beaver castor, oil of anise, and a variety of other substances. The formula, with exact measurements, had been perfected by Allan's father and grandfather. Far from merely smelling, it reeked. But foxes and coyotes found it irresistible.

Allan made a mental check to see if he'd forgotten anything, decided he hadn't, put the bottle of scent in the basket, and shrugged into the shoulder straps. The various articles in the basket, the basket itself, and Allan's gloves, had first been de-scented by leaving them for three months in a hollow stump. They had then been put in a cage with three captive foxes so that fox scent might impregnate them. Finally they had been stored in the shed and left strictly alone until needed. Trapping was always hard work, but taking pelts in autumn was a lazy man's job compared to trapping in deep snow.

Lacing the snowshoes to his pacs, Allan followed

his own trail back across the lake, toward the mouth of Balsam Creek. Because the snow was broken by his previous tracks, he made far better time than he had yesterday. Stormy, following behind, experienced less trouble too. Allan looked back and spoke encouragingly, but did not touch the big dog; there must be no alien scent on his gloves.

Frost crystals glittered in the rising sun. Allan turned his cheek away from the little wind that blew, and wished he'd thought to look at his thermometer. It was, he guessed, about twenty-five degrees below zero. That was cold, but right for travelling. The snow was crisp and packed easily.

At the mouth of Balsam Creek, Allan left the beaten trail and fought through unbroken snow toward the overhanging ledge beneath which mink travelled. Before he reached it, he turned and spoke to Stormy.

"Sit!" he commanded.

Immediately the big dog sat in the snowshoe trail, and Allan went on alone. Reaching the ledge, he knelt to see the tracks of two mink in the dusting of snow that had sifted beneath it. Six feet beyond was a small hole where they'd tunneled into snow to reach the ice labyrinth that coated Balsam Creek. Allan used the blade of his de-scented axe to scrape aside the snow and sand beneath the ledge. He took one of the smaller traps from his basket, set it, staked it to a chunk of wood, and sifted sand over the trap with his gloved hands. Finally, trying to make everything appear exactly as it had been, he replaced the snow, back-tracked to where Stormy waited, gave him permission to rise, and continued up the ice.

Suddenly and without warning he was pulled forcibly backward to a sitting position. For a moment he remained too astonished to move, then felt Stormy's big head over his shoulder and Stormy's breath warm on his cheek. Allan was annoyed; why had Stormy upset him by grabbing his jacket and pulling him backward? He turned to reprimand the dog.

Just as he did, there was a loud cracking up the creek ahead of them. The snow settled perceptibly. Thirty seconds later, a whole section of ice collapsed and the slow waters of Balsam Creek showed black against the snow.

Allan wiped his suddenly sweating brow with his sleeve. Had he been on that ice, he could not have helped falling with it. Doubtless he'd have got out again; at this point Balsam Creek was only about three feet deep and nowhere were its waters swift. But if the creek were ten or more feet deep and *did* have a swift current . . .

Allan looked perplexedly at his dog. He himself had been wholly unaware of danger, but Stormy had known. However, the senses of the dullest animal shame those of the keenest human. There had been some sign, a faint preliminary cracking that Allan hadn't heard but Stormy had, or perhaps a quivering of the ice, that had warned the dog.

"Who's teaching *me* to sit?" Allan said with a feeble grin.

He cut at right angles into the forest, detoured

around the break, and continued up Balsam Creek with new confidence. The Beaver Flowage was not without its dangers and he would be a fool to ignore them, but just having Stormy along minimized those perils.

The next trap was a fox set some distance back in the forest. Allan swerved to it, and Stormy sat companionably near while his master dug. It was hard work, and as he dug, Allan thought of the many tales he'd read that made trapping sound like a romantic profession. He reached the spot where he thought he'd set the trap, missed by fifteen inches, and probed into the snow until he found it. As he'd expected, the trap was frozen.

Allan picked up the drag, a block of wood to which the chain was attached, and slammed the trap against a tree. He slammed it again. This time, with a metallic click of its steel jaws, the trap snapped shut, the action forcing the frozen snow out of the working parts. Carrying the trap by its drag, Allan snowshoed on through the forest. A hundred yards from where he'd picked up the trap, he made Stormy sit again and back-tracked thirty feet through a thicket. Unrolling his strip of canvas, he unlaced his snowshoes and crept out on the canvas.

Foxes never do anything the hard way if they can find an easy one. Rather than undergo the work of breaking its own trail, any fox travelling this thicket would be quick to use the already-broken snowshoe trail. The fact that a man and dog had made the initial path would mean nothing, for the fox's nose would tell him exactly how long ago they had passed and that neither was present now. He'd still be alert. Any foreign object, the slightest hint of a trap, would send even an inexperienced fox scooting into the snow to one side.

Again Allan scooped a hole with his de-scented hatchet and very carefully lined it with tissue paper. He set the trap, laid it on the paper, and buried chain and drag in the snow. Then he covered the set trap with more paper. He let a single drop from his scent bottle fall onto the upper layer of paper and replaced the snow exactly as he had found it. Finally, rolling up the canvas as he went backward, he rejoined Stormy.

The set he'd left behind was not ideal; when snow lay deep in the Beaver Flowage there was no such thing as an ideal man-designed trap. But it was good. The tissue paper below and above would keep the trap from freezing. If Allan had done his work correctly, and left no sign other than that a man and dog had come this way, any fox that decided to use the snowshoe trail would smell the scent and might be caught.

Allan dug out and re-set three more traps, then swung away from the creek and came to a balsam swamp where deer were winter-yarded. He saw them flee as he approached, running down paths they themselves had beaten toward concealing thickets. This was still late autumn and all the deer he saw were in good shape; obviously they were getting enough to eat. But as winter progressed and available food was consumed, all would be hungry. By the time the spring sun ate into the snowdrifts, there would be numerous dead deer in this swamp for there simply was not enough food for all. Foxes, coyotes, and other carnivores that always haunted such a place as deer began to die, would be rolling in fat.

Man himself was to blame for that, Allan reflected bitterly. Over-zealous to protect deer, which he wanted for his own hunting pleasure, man had eliminated many four-footed hunters that normally preyed upon deer and in consequence had succeeded in establishing large herds. Now, for the most part, there was only man to keep the herds in check. This resulted in too many deer for the available range. Allan thought suddenly of a magazine story he'd read.

It was an impassioned and over-sentimentalized plea for wildlife and at the same time a vitriolic denunciation of hunters. The author painted vivid word pictures of wild creatures shot down. He called deer "the forest's innocents," and railed about the viciousness of shooting them with firearms. Allan decided as he walked along that he would like to bring that author to this yard about the middle of March and let him see for himself what happened to many of "the forest's innocents" when there was too little browse to go around. A bullet offered a far kinder death than slow starvation. If deer were harvested sensibly rather than sentimentally, a fair share of those that died every winter anyhow would provide valuable food for humans.

Leaving the deer yard, Allan swerved toward a grove of bushy balsams that surrounded a pond.

Due to some natural phenomenon, this pond never froze. Shiners and chubs swarmed in it, mink came to hunt them, and Allan hunted the mink.

He came to where he had left a trap, and gave a troubled frown. Trap and drag were gone, and there were no tracks, so whatever had been caught was trapped before the recent snow. There was not a sign to tell where it had gone, and Allan felt a little sick. To lose an animal in this fashion, to consign it to a usually lingering death, always made him wish that he might find another way to earn necessary money.

Suddenly, out in the balsams, Stormy barked. Allan whirled, unaware until he looked that the dog was gone. Then he hurried back, found the trail Stormy had left, and followed it to where the big dog sat at the foot of a dead balsam.

Eight feet up in the tree, baleful eyes fixed on Stormy, sat a big lynx with the missing trap on a front paw. Even as he drew his revolver from its sheath, Allan knew that this lynx might have run until the trap chain snagged, then easily pulled free. But lynx and wildcats seldom fight traps, and there are various theories why. Allan himself believed the reason to be that a cat's complex nervous system rebels at the least pain, and where a coyote or wolf would have fought the trap, the lynx had treed.

Allan drew his revolver, aimed carefully, and tumbled the lynx in the snow. Even as he did, it occurred to Allan that he was false to his own precepts; this lynx was a predator that was probably hanging around the yards in hopes of killing a sick or weak deer. But there would be more predators, and one more or less could not make a great deal of difference.

He ran forward to retrieve his prize. Probably he would not take a more valuable pelt all winter, and the chances were excellent that he'd have missed it without Stormy. Allan looked at the big dog gratefully.

"I've got me a real partner!" he exulted. "I sure enough have!"

6. The Big Pike

Stormy slept in his favorite spot along the wall, and his paws twitched as he dreamed happy canine dreams of some good thing that was happening. Allan used the tip of his finger to rub a hole in the frosted windowpane, looked at the thermometer hanging just outside, and saw that it was nine below zero.

The winter had been long and bitter. Most of the time the sky was cloudy, and rarely were there three consecutive days without a storm. There had been nearly two weeks when the temperature had fallen to fifty below and risen no higher than twenty below. The north wind blew almost constantly, and Allan had a struggle to keep his trapline trails open.

In their yards deer died by the score, and carnivores that normally prowled for food had all but forsaken the hunt to live off the carcasses of these unfortunate beasts. Cottontail rabbits and splay-footed snowshoe hares, venturing out to nibble whatever they could find, fell in vast numbers to an inundation of snowy owls that had come down from the arctic. Only the chickadees seemed happy. Their feathers ruffled against the cold, they flitted about the willows that thrust above snowdrifts and sang constantly, and always cheerfully, of warm suns and spring weather that couldn't possibly be far away.

Stormy raised his head and blinked sleepy eyes as Allan went to the table, sat down, and began to study the dog-eared notebook in which he kept accounts. In a hard winter such as this, his catch of furs should have been negligible. But the book assured him that he had fifty-two foxes, eleven coyotes, three lynx, thirty-three mink, and sixty-nine weasels. It was more fur than he usually took even in a mild winter, when trapping conditions were far better than they were now. As Allan turned the pages he thought back over how this had come to pass.

Stormy was directly responsible for a great deal of it. The big dog had an uncanny nose for scent plus a powerful hunting instinct and great intelligence. Many times, when Allan would have gone past without ever knowing anything was there, Stormy had pointed out some furtive, hidden lair or trail or fur animal. Two of the three lynx had not been trapped at all; Stormy had treed them and held them until Allan came. The dog's nose had found every animal that made off with trap and drag; for the first time since he'd been trapping, Allan had not lost one such pelt. Stormy had run down and caught seven of the foxes while they floundered in deep snow.

In a very few lessons, he had mastered and would obey the basic commands of sit, down, heel, and stay. Stormy had taught himself about traps by stepping into one. But rather than panic, as many dogs did when trapped, he had waited patiently for Allan to help him. Stormy had rebelled only when Allan tried to put a collar around his neck; he wanted no bonds of any description.

Actually, he needed none. Allan remembered the first time he had gone away and left the big dog loose at home. Somewhat fearfully, Allan had ordered him to stay at the house while he went to Tillotson for supplies and to see his father at Laceyville. Instead of following, as Allan had thought he might, Stormy had seemed perfectly content to stay and was asleep on the porch when Allan returned.

Allan rested his head on his hands and gave himself to day dreaming.

His father was back, the feud with the Torrances was amicably settled, and once again there was highway access across Joe Torrance's farm. The bunkhouse overflowed with hunters, and their main topic of conversation was not the game they'd bagged, but Stormy's amazing performances. They were so impressed with the big dog that all reserved a place for next season and told the Marleys that they really must build another bunkhouse. Allan and his father made so much money that they could give up trapping. After following the waterfowl in flight south and seeing for themselves the winter homes of the ducks and geese that visited them every spring and autumn, they came home and spent the rest of the winter on various experiments to save starving deer.

Allan shook himself out of his dream. Life was not yet that rosy, but definitely it was not all grim. His winter's take of fur meant money, and money meant that he might continue to live without constantly dipping into the tin box under the floor. There was a chance that the evil genie which had sprung full grown out of his father's fight with old Bert Torrance would yet be foiled.

He listened to the wind driving snow against the windows and sighed wistfully. Suddenly he yearned for trees in leaf, sunshine on green grass, and arrowhead and pickerelweed in bloom. Then he put the wish out of his mind. No one knew how long winter in the Beaver Flowage might last. Whoever decided to make his home there automatically made an unwritten contract with the elements to accept the seasons as they came.

Banking the fire, Allan climbed into bed, pulled the wool blankets up around his chin, and fell asleep to the sound of the wind.

He did not know when he awakened, but the night was still so black that he could just barely see the windows. He pushed the blankets aside and raised himself on one elbow, while a throbbing excitement pulsed through his whole body. He strained for a repetition of a sound that he seemed to have heard in his sleep. It came again; he *had* heard it!

Drifting out of the black sky, it was a far-carrying and haunting cry. The first hairy man who heard that sound had tilted his head to search out its source, and it has touched a sensitive chord in human beings ever since. It was the voice of freedom unlimited, the incarnation of nature itself, the sound and song of fond dreams: the cry of the northbound wild geese.

Entranced, Allan listened until the geese passed

in the night and were heard no more. Then he leaped from his bed, ran barefooted across the floor, and jerked the door open. Stormy came to join him. For a long interval, both remained under the spell of this notice that a magical change had been wrought.

The wind had at last shifted to the south. Already the snow on the roof was melting, and water dripped from the eaves. Allan smiled dreamily, then stooped to encircle Stormy's neck with his right arm. He was blissfully happy. Spring in other places might send its advance messengers in the form of crocuses, robins, and small boys with kites. But wild geese winging north and talking to each other about their journey was the only message for him.

He wondered if his father had heard it.

Stormy sprawled on the ground beside him, Allan sat on the lower step of his front porch. For the moment all that was worthwhile and desirable in life consisted of being lazy and soaking up sunshine. Half asleep, he was further lulled by the rhythmic pattern of wavelets set in motion by the balmy breeze that stirred the lake. It would be a good day to visit the islands, but right now he felt too lazy.

The lake's two islands each bore a growth of willow brush that every winter was flattened and ground by ice cakes tossed up by wind-lashed waters, and every summer sprang up again. There was a knoll or crest in the very center of the larger island, and upon it grew a single tall aspen that so far had resisted winter winds. Allan knew that a close inspection of either island would reveal a tangle of

broken and bruised willows, a forbidding and unat-
tractive thicket. But green leaves had already
sprouted on the live willow canes that remained, and
leaflets dangled from the aspen so that, from this
distance, both islands were softly beautiful.

It was the part of wisdom, Allan thought dreamily,
not to look too closely into things at times. When one
did, faults became glaringly apparent. But if he kept
his distance, he saw only the virtues, as with the
islands. Allan grinned at his own homespun philos-
ophy, clasped both hands behind his head, and
leaned back against an upper step.

The wild geese that had flown over that winter's
night, talking as they flew, had indeed proved true
forerunners of spring. The thaw had followed in earnest, and only by fighting his way through slush had
Allan been able to reach and gather up his traps.
How had the geese known?

They were not, as some claimed, always infallible;
Allan himself had known of geese that became
stormbound. But their errors were few. Led by an
experienced old goose or gander, a flock usually
consisted of the parent birds, their young of the season, and perhaps some of the children's children. Or
several families might flock together for the long
journey south in autumn and north in spring. How
did they get their advance weather reports, so winter
always followed the southbound geese and spring
the northbound?

Thinking back, Allan remembered that for a whole
day after the first geese flew over, there had been no
other northbound migrants. Then eight mallards had

dipped out of the sky, braked themselves with set wings, and settled on a puddle of melted snow water out on the ice. They had been followed by a pair of pintails and a flock of green-winged teal.

With the arrival of the teal, the dam broke.

Day and night, long V-lines of geese were in the air. Every hour of the twenty-four resounded to their honking. All were bound for nesting sites and many would find them in Canada's wonderful waterland to the north. But many geese, and a great variety of ducks, sought home sites in the Beaver Flowage. Though Allan had never been anywhere else to see for himself, he thought that waterfowl must nest both sides of the Canadian border along all major flyways.

Two years ago Allan had found a nest of ducks which he had never before seen, and finally identified as Pacific eiders. Their presence was puzzling, for Pacific eiders prefer to nest on the sea coast. But they had been no harder to explain than the occasional pink-footed goose, white-faced tree duck, Bahama pintail, or other non-native waterfowl that visited the Beaver Flowage. Their presence was a fascinating puzzle.

Did sudden, furious gales blow them from their usual migration routes? Did enemies force them to veer this far from any haunts they knew? Was it possible that some waterfowl, like some people, have twisted brains? Rather than migrate with their fellows, did these aliens veer off at an angle and end up here? Or were they merely born adventurers who wanted to try something new?

Even though he knew there must be some other

answer, Allan liked this last surmise. Certainly any waterfowl that braved a wide expanse of stormy sea found adventure in plenty.

As he lazed in the sun, Allan suddenly felt rich. It was not his winter catch of furs, nor the seventy muskrat pelts he had added in the early spring, nor the good price he had received for his furs. Rather, he felt like a king surveying his wealthy kingdom. Even as the thought occurred to him, he decided that no mere king had ever had so much. Allan rose, stretched, and addressed Stormy.

"Come on. Guess the king had better add another diamond to the crown jewels. That's you."

Stormy padding beside him, he made his way to the lake shore and looked down at a craft he had drawn up there. Properly it was a skiff, but fundamentally it was a work of art and skiff was far too crude a title. It was a Marley skiff, designed and built by Allan's father exclusively for duck hunting. Ten feet over all, both ends were blunted. There were two seats, each wide enough for one man, and a paddle rather than oars furnished motive power. It was so light that one man could carry it easily. It drew so little water that, with a man on each seat and a dog in the bow, it would float and could be maneuvered in the shallowest water. Easy to handle, a man could paddle it all day and never feel tired. At the same time, it was seaworthy enough to ride the heaviest waves. But it was a lady through and through and demanded the respect accorded such. Whoever treated a Marley skiff properly could go safely wherever there was water. Whoever did not was destined for a ducking.

Allan pushed the skiff out just far enough so that its bow remained on the lake shore. He looked speculatively at Stormy, then removed his shoes and socks. As a further precautionary measure he stripped off his shirt and the upper part of his underwear. When he called, Stormy came immediately and waded with him as Allan shoved the skiff out just far enough to float.

"Get in, Stormy," he ordered.

Stormy flattened his ears and looked puzzled. Steadying the skiff with one hand, Allan lifted both Stormy's front paws over the side. Stooping, he shoved his shoulder against the big dog's rear and boosted him into the skiff. At the same time he spoke firmly.

"Stay."

Stormy stood with all four paws wide apart and braced. His ears drooped and his eyes rolled. He'd swim the lake a dozen times if he wanted to and enjoy every swim, but this he neither knew nor trusted.

"Sit!" Allan ordered.

Stormy sat, and because he was too far to one side, the skiff tilted in the shallow water. Allan pulled him back to the center and stepped cautiously into the rear paddler's seat. He dipped his paddle lightly, and like the sensitive craft she was, the skiff responded. With one cautious eye on Stormy, Allan kept to shallow water near shore. He grinned sympathetically. Stormy continued to sit with fore legs spread and stiff, and acted as though any moment might be his last. But true to his training, he sat very still.

Allan thought ahead to the waterfowl season that would come before another winter closed in. If he and Stormy were to hunt ducks together, Stormy must learn how to ride in a skiff. The only way to teach him how to do so was to take him riding.

After ten minutes, Allan swung out into the lake. Light as a puff of thistledown on a summer's breeze, the skiff rode a swell. Allan's confidence grew.

"How about this, Stormy?" he called happily.

Stormy turned his head, moved slightly, and as though an unseen arm had given it a sudden shove, the skiff rolled over. Hanging to his paddle, Allan went down, kicked up through the water, hooked his right arm over the skiff's hull and shifted the paddle to that hand. Stormy swam up to him, looking so blissful at being in the water that Allan burst out laughing.

"Me and my big mouth! If I'd shut up, you wouldn't have moved!"

Allan twined his free hand in loose skin on Stormy's neck. Towing both his master and the skiff, the big dog struck for shore. There Allan lifted the skiff across his knees, emptied it, and set it right side up.

"All right," he said. "We'll try again."

Twice more Stormy upset the skiff, but on the fourth try he found both his sea legs and his balance and began to enjoy this novel method of travel. From then on he stood, head into the wind and smirking in his own fashion as he swayed from side to side to offset every lurch of the skiff. Again he had proved his ability to learn.

Satisfied with the dog's behavior, Allan paddled toward the mouth of Balsam Creek. Responsive to the slightest dip of the paddle, the skiff handled as easily as a fine canoe. A little way up the creek, Allan slowed and let the skiff drift.

On the opposite bank stood a duck, a pompous little creature whose predominating plumage was brown and reddish brown. It had an absurd fantail, a cockily tilted head, and somehow imparted the impression that it was ruler of its world.

It was a ruddy drake, one of the smaller of its kind and easily the worst-tempered. Allan searched the grass and, a short distance from the drake, discovered the duck trying to make herself invisible by holding still and crouching as low as possible. Obviously she was nesting.

Allan watched the domestic scene with pleasure. For all their pompousness and temper, ruddy ducks were his favorites. The drake was the only one of the entire duck family that, rather than leave after the mating season, stayed to guard his mate while she brooded and helped rear the ducklings after they hatched. It seemed a lucky omen because this pair was nesting on Balsam Creek.

About to resume paddling, Allan dropped his glance to the shallow water just below the alert drake, and saw what at first seemed to be a submerged log. Then he made out the head, body, and tail of a giant pike and caught his breath. He looked away, sure that he had exaggerated the pike's size, but when he glanced back he knew that he had not.

The little drake and his mate would fight furiously for their brood and if necessary give their own lives. But nothing the size of a ruddy duck could even hope to fight the monster that awaited. As soon as the ducklings took to the water, the pike would get them, and then very likely finish off with the parents. Allan waved a hand at the angry drake.

"I'll see what I can do about it, pal," he promised.

He turned and paddled home so fast that spray curled over either side of the skiff's bow, much to Stormy's delight.

7. Ugly Incident

Lying in bed and giving half an ear to the whisper of a gentle spring rain, Allan was both wakeful and anxious. Every day, with Stormy as passenger, he'd paddled up Balsam Creek to the ruddy ducks' nest. He'd cast every lure in his tackle box with which he'd ever taken a pike, then every one he thought might take a pike, and had finally resorted to soaking chubs in the big pike's lair.

He'd caught all the pike he and Stormy could eat. But he hadn't provoked a single rise from the giant he wanted, and as far as Allan was concerned, he thought he knew why. Regardless of those who claim that fish have no intelligence as that overworked term is generally understood, it remained Allan's unshakable opinion that big ones grow big because they're also smart. The giant pike was simply too clever to strike a lure or take a bait.

It was very troublesome, for according to Allan's tally the ducklings were scheduled to leave their nest within the next couple of days. He might, he told himself, shrug it off with the knowledge that thousands and tens of thousands of ducklings fell to predatory fish every season, and that these few more would make no difference. But they did make a difference.

Long ago, hordes of waterfowl literally choked every flyway. They were preyed upon by natural enemies and a few primitive men, but the combined toll taken by both made scarcely a dent on the vast flocks. Then came civilization. Besides slaughtering millions of ducks and geese by every method his ingenuity could devise, modern man invaded ancient breeding and feeding grounds. Millions of acres of marsh land that had provided both nesting sites and food had been drained and converted to agriculture and other uses. Meanwhile, slaughter continued with such fury that at one time all the waterfowl in America were in real danger of extermination.

Only a few far-sighted people appreciated the true situation. Fighting every inch of the way against market hunters and thoughtless sportsmen, stubborn conservationists finally gained their objectives. The remaining breeding grounds were given protection. Wherever it was feasible, marshes and ponds were restored in areas where they had been drained. Rigid bag limits were established. Since waterfowl are migratory, and thus not permanently resident in any one state or province, responsibility for their well-being was invested in the Federal Government. Gradually the flocks recovered to a point where all who loved waterfowl hunting might have an opportunity to enjoy it. The future of the waterfowl now depended largely upon those who hunted them, as Allan well knew. Though he probably could have shot as many ducks as he pleased without being found out, Allan always restricted himself to the legal limit. If he could save the ruddy duck's brood, he felt in a sense he would be replacing a measure of the toll he took of other ducks.

But he admitted honestly that there was another factor involved. He took great pride in his angling skill, and the fact that the monster pike had flouted his most expertly cast lure had wounded that pride sorely. Well, he'd try it again tomorrow.

The next morning he tied a new wire leader to his casting line, bent it double, and tested it for possible weaknesses by snapping it smartly straight. Pike are armed with formidable teeth, and though Allan had taken many on standard gut leaders and found great sport in so doing, he'd lost too many pike because they bit through the gut. This time he wanted to be sure. Next he sorted his lures and finally chose three. They were battered, toothmarked, and not one of the three had more than streaks of the original paint remaining. But they took pike when nothing else would. Finally Allan tested the point of his gaff, found it sharp enough to suit him, and gathered up his tackle.

Stormy, whose liking for boat rides had become near passion, pranced happily beside Allan as he made his way to the lake. The dog waited impatiently for his master to float the skiff, then waded out and, scarcely rocking the sensitive little craft, jumped into his proper place in the bow. Allan took the rear paddler's seat and they were off.

They crossed the lake at top speed, but as he entered Balsam Creek, Allan slowed. He knew that the ruddys had become so accustomed to his presence that they practically ignored him. But with babies to protect the ducks were now doubly anxious, and Allan had no wish to panic the brood. Nor did he want to alarm the pike. He let the skiff glide to a halt below the nest and looked up the bank.

The drake, proud and pompous as ever, glanced briefly at the skiff and at once turned his attention back to his family. A cluster of ducklings at her feet, the duck stood near the nesting site, fussing over her offspring. Allan tried to count the ducklings, thought there were fourteen, and was a little surprised. The tiny ruddy lays larger eggs than do other species twice her size, and her normal clutch is from six to ten eggs. Obviously this particular ruddy was content with nothing except a superior performance.

Allan relaxed; the ducks obviously still considered him harmless. The skiff drifted downstream. Dipping his paddle, Allan sent it back to where he could get a better view of the family.

Led by the drake and trailed by the duck, the whole family descended the grassy bank to water level. The drake waded in and started swimming. As though this were something to which they were well accustomed, and not a wholly new element, the ducklings followed with no hesitation at all. The mother duck brought up the rear. Within a few minutes, their downy behinds bobbing like so many corks, the ducklings began to probe for food beneath the water.

Allan watched, wholly entranced. Most ducklings whose parents normally tip for food feed entirely from the surface until, probably partly by instinct and partly from the example their parents set, they learn to tip too. Ruddy ducklings are one of the very few that know almost from the minute they enter the water that they'll find food beneath it.

So intent was he on the duck family that Allan almost missed the swirl in the water. It was little more than a ripple, but when Allan counted again, there were only thirteen ducklings. The little drake turned furiously to attack the danger, but he could see nothing to attack.

Allan reached for his casting rod, wondering about the fussy habits of this pike. The adult ducks must have been feeding on Balsam Creek since building their nest. The giant pike could have swallowed both, but it hadn't. Probably, after appeasing its winter hunger, the pike had become a gourmet. Full-feathered ducks would be acceptable when it was really hungry, but ducklings were a delicacy any time.

Allan cast, saw his plug strike the water six feet from the duck, and started the retrieve. He was still reeling in when the water swirled again and another duckling disappeared. Allan muttered under his breath.

The pike knew what it wanted, and what it wanted was ducklings. It would pay no attention to anything else as long as those tender morsels were in sight. Still, Allan had to try. He cast again, trying to come nearer to where he thought the pike was lurking. Just as the lure left the tip of his rod, the furious little drake swerved and changed course. The plug splashed eighteen inches beyond him, but slack line settled over his back. Allan held his breath. He'd hoped to bring help to the duck family, but it looked as though he might easily bring tragedy instead. To retrieve now almost certainly meant that he would set his lure in the drake, with possible serious injury. Allan sighed with relief when the line slid from the valiant little warrior's back. In doing so, the line brushed a duckling.

Then a case of dynamite exploded at the end of Allan's line and the battle was joined.

Even as he raised his rod so it could take some strain off his line, Allan knew both that he had hooked the giant pike and that the doing was wholly accidental. The monster had not struck the lure. Its objective had been the duckling brushed by the line and the lure had simply been in its way. But regardless of how it had happened, the pike was still hooked. It surged upstream and the rod bowed as Allan paid line out. Then the pike swapped directions to come downstream and Allan reeled furiously to keep a tight line. He stole a quick glance at the duck family, now fifty yards upstream and still moving. Then Allan gave all his attention to the battle.

Lacking the snap and dash of a hooked trout or bass, the pike more than made up in size and sheer strength anything it might be missing in spirit. The hooked fish darted under the skiff, and Allan breathed his relief when it came back out. The eight-pound-test casting line was brand new, but if a fish this size snagged it, it would snap like a thread.

Giving line where he must, reeling furiously when

he could, Allan played his fish. Presently the savage rushes began to shorten, but Allan didn't know whether five or forty-five minutes had passed. Then, ten feet from the skiff's side, Allan saw the pike, the plug hooked securely in its lower jaw. It came to within six inches of the surface, then bored back down. Allan let it go. But he knew now that, barring accidents and errors, he had won this battle. He shortened his line, brought the pike up a second time, but could not stop its going back down. Then, finally, he had it alongside the skiff.

Allan moved with great care, for all the angling skill at his command was needed right now. Many a hooked fish, brought to boatside, has been sent surging away in fresh panic and lost through a clumsy stab of gaff or net. Moving cautiously, Allan slid his gaff over the side, turned the hook, and set it with all his strength. The skiff rocked alarmingly as he drew the pike over the side, disengaged the gaff, turned it, and subdued the flapping pike with the heavy handle.

Sinking back in the seat, Allan noticed for the first time that he was perspiring freely. He wiped his face with his sleeve and found that he was shaking. Well, he had something to shake about. He had heard old-timers speak nostalgically of pike up to fifty pounds, and probably there had been some. But as old-timers aged, he noticed that the fish they'd caught in earlier years had a tendency to grow. Allan estimated the length of this pike as forty inches and thought it weighed nearly a pound for every inch.

That was a nice fish in anybody's time. Not in Allan's memory had the Beaver Flowage produced as big a pike. He beamed at Stormy.

"Look at him!"

Stormy, to whom fish were fish regardless of whether they were four or forty inches long, was visibly unimpressed. But Allan's smile widened as he surveyed his catch.

In the not-too-distant past pike were considered vermin, and nobody cared about them. But of late years, with the supply of fishermen bidding fair to outstrip the supply of fish, a determined effort had been launched to call attention to the very real game qualities of the once-despised pike. Annually, with the subtle intention of luring as many pre-season vacationists as possible, the Tillotson Chamber of Commerce sponsored a Spring Pike Derby and offered a hundred dollar cash award for the biggest pike brought in.

Allan looked once more at the monster turning glassy-eyed in his skiff and knew who would win this year.

An empty pack on his back for supplies and the carefully wrapped pike in his hands, Allan fairly bounded across Joe Torrance's land. He saw Joe, almost waved at him, and walked on, grinning to himself. Nothing, not even the Torrances, could be wrong today. Allan started to whistle.

The pike, as he had determined when he got home, was just over forty-three inches long and weighed thirty-eight pounds. Wrapping it in wet cloth, Allan had ordered Stormy to stay home and started at once for Tillotson.

As he entered the village, Allan saw that it had not yet completely emerged from winter hibernation but was awakening fast. Motel and trailer park owners were painting and raking, and a couple of the more optimistic were even cutting grass. Every motel seemed to have at least one guest and there were five or six cars at some. These would be fishermen, for the first of June, when the vacation season officially opened, was still five weeks away. But if early signs were any criterion, the Beaver Flowage was in for a prosperous season.

Tempted to stop and show his prize to Jeff Darnley, the game warden, Allan changed his mind and went on. The great pike was sure to set Tillotson buzzing, and maximum effect probably would be achieved by taking it to Johnny Malaming's and letting the news spread from there. Secretary-treasurer and general spark plug of the Tillotson Chamber of Commerce, and never one to miss any bets, Johnny froze the biggest entrants in the Spring Pike Derby inside blocks of ice, displayed them in his front window, and as a result did a land-office business in fishing tackle.

J. Malaming's Great Emporium was ready for the expected influx of tourists. A rack of cane poles stood beside the door. The front windows were filled with a gorgeous array of lures, most of which appealed more to fishermen than they did to fish. Ruth Callaman, Johnny's pretty young niece and no small attraction insofar as men customers were concerned, was there to help him through the summer season.

Allan entered, and was exchanging a little friendly banter with Ruth when Johnny came from the rear of the store.

"Goshamighty!" he exploded. "I thought you'd stepped in a puddle, got your feet wet, and been settin' by the stove these past three months!"

"It was only two months," Allan said mildly. "How've things been?"

"Poorly," Johnny lamented. "Poorly. An honest storekeeper can't hardly make a livin' any more."

"What do you know about honest storekeepers?" Allan retorted. "Got something to show you, Johnny."

He unwrapped the pike, held it up, and for the first time in his life saw Johnny Malaming speechless. But not for long.

"Nice fish," Johnny grunted calmly. "But when—"

"Yeah!" Allan jeered. "But when you were a boy you used this kind for bait! How about entering it in the Derby?"

"Can do," Johnny agreed with more enthusiasm.

Angelo Antonelli, Tillotson's barber, came in and looked excitedly at the pike. Then came Tom Montgomery, who owned the hardware store. He was followed by Hapley Jackson, better known as Slap Happy Jackie, the local bum. The store filled quickly, with everyone who entered voicing a different theory as to how and where the pike had been caught.

"You say a Marley caught that fish?" said a heavy, skeptical voice.

"Yep, young Allan Marley," Johnny Malaming answered.

"He did, eh?" The voice was loud, thick, insulting. "Bet he speared it!"

The owner of the voice was a tall and handsome young man with a reckless air of deviltry. He was Bob Torrance, Joe's younger brother and the only member of the clan who had forsaken his native home. A merchant seaman, he was often gone for long periods. But he always returned to Tillotson with pockets full of money and stayed until it was spent. Very recently, Allan decided, he'd been spending his money for something besides milk.

"Marley here?" the voice demanded.

"Right over there."

Bob Torrance elbowed his way to Allan. "Din' you spear that pike?"

"No."

"Tha's a lie!" the sailor accused. "You're jus' like your ol' man. Wanna fight?"

Allan said nothing. There was no point in arguing with a man who was already two-thirds drunk.

"Yellow, huh? Jus' what I thought!"

"That's enough, Bob."

Enoch Carew and Alfred Devlin, Torrance cousins, took the sailor's arms and steered him toward the door. But he hurled one more challenge as he went out.

"See ya some day, Marley! See ya down by your lake! We may have the lil' fight yet!"

8. Summer Doings

An embarrassed silence took possession of what had been an eager, interested crowd. They'd gathered to look at a record fish, which they considered everybody's business, and had been interrupted by a quarrel that didn't concern them. Still, it seemed strange that the insults of the drunken sailor hadn't made Allan take a poke at him. A couple of the bystanders directed contemptuous glances at Allan, and Slap Happy Jackie, the town bum, smirked openly. It was plain that some of the crowd thought him a coward.

Allan's anger flared. He was not afraid of Bob or any other Torrance, he knew that. But he didn't want any more trouble, and had promised his father there wouldn't be. Thinking of his father quieted his anger; now he only wanted to get away.

"Guess I'd better get my order," he told Johnny.

"Sure thing," Johnny said understandingly. "What'll it be?"

Still embarrassed, the crowd in the store slipped quietly out while Allan was ordering. As Johnny produced the various articles, Allan stowed them carefully in his pack. Then he paid for his supplies, shouldered the pack, and swung to leave.

"I'll see you."

Ruth said viciously, "One of these days some-body's going to take that big ape apart."

"I guess so, Ruth," Allan murmured dispiritedly.

"I'm not blaming you, Allan. It's fine of you to refuse to hit a drunk."

"They're the kind to hit," Allan retorted, manag-ing a feeble grin. "They fall easier."

Johnny indicated the pike. "I'm goin' to freeze that baby in a cake of ice and put him in the window. You've sure got the award sewed up."

Allan grinned again. "*Now* you admit it. So long, you two."

As soon as he was outside the store, he had a curious feeling that Tillotson's population had in-creased ten times, and that every eye was riveted on him. Whispered conversations seemed to echo in his ears: "There he goes. That's Allan Marley. He's big enough, isn't he?" "Husky enough, too, but he wouldn't fight, eh?" "Nope, not even when Bob Torrance insulted him." "He must be yellow."

Allan walked on, knowing that every eye did not follow him and that the conversations occurred only in his own fancy. Besides, he had plenty of friends in Tillotson and the least they'd do was to hear both sides before making any decisions about him. But the illusion that he was being laughed out of town remained so strong that only with an effort was he able to hold himself to a walk.

Beyond Tillotson's limits, he felt no better; cars going both ways seemed to slow just to look at him. Only when he left the highway and started down the freeway that led to his lake did he begin to breathe easier. He told himself that nobody should have hit Bob Torrance, though a couple of slaps would have done him good. But he hadn't even slapped him. Was he really afraid of the Torrances? Was it just an excuse when he kept telling himself that fighting could only lead to trouble, and that trouble was something the Marleys had enough of?

Allan walked swiftly, full of his conflicting thoughts. When he came to Joe Torrance's farm, he averted his eyes from the house and outbuildings. If Bob Torrance was at Joe's, he didn't want to see him. He wanted only to reach his lake, and forget the whole business. But he was halted by a shout, and saw Joe Torrance hurrying toward him. Wanting to go on, to run if necessary, Allan forced himself to wait.

Of medium height and build, Joe had the powerful chest and muscled arms that are usually found on men who do heavy farm work every day. He was hot, and his curly black hair was plastered tightly against his head. There was no friendliness in his brown eyes.

"Did Bob brace you?" he demanded.

"Yes." Allan hoped he sounded cool.

"Did you hit him?"

Allan's face flushed. "Did he come home alone?"

"No. Enoch and Al brought him."

"Then why don't you ask them what happened?"

"I did."

"Then you know Bob's drunk again and that I didn't hit him."

"That's what Enoch and Al told me, but Bob keeps saying he fought you and you ran. He says he's going to come finish it."

"Don't let him," Allan said shortly.

"I'll keep him here if I can, but don't mess with him if he comes. Not now or any other time."

"I'll decide what to do, and when," Allan flared.

"Don't be an ass!" Joe snapped. "I'm just giving you fair advance warning that I'll finish any trouble you start. But I won't start it and you needn't if you'll just let Bob talk. He wouldn't be this way unless—"

"Unless he was drunk all the time," Allan finished cruelly.

Allan turned on his heel and, without looking back, strode on toward the lake. His sudden surge of anger made him realize that he had plenty of Marley temper himself, and that his father had been right to make him promise to avoid trouble. Then he became aware that Joe Torrance was yelling at him.

"You pig-headed Marleys are all tarred with the same brush! You got no sense or reason! If you tried to get along with people, you might find you could do it!"

As he continued down the freeway, Allan thought seriously of going to Cardsville and looking for work. If he stayed here or got a job in Tillotson, there'd be trouble, no matter how he tried to avoid it. The money he could earn would enable him to keep going until his father was released, and then— But what about Stormy? He couldn't take the dog to Cardsville.

He reached the end of the freeway, where he had

left his skiff. Allan stowed his pack in the bow, launched the skiff, and started down the lake.

As soon as he was on the water, its powerful bonds began to pull at him; there was no longer any question about leaving. This was home as no other land ever could be, and aside from its pull on him, he owed it something. His grandfather had come to this lake with no assets besides his axe, his gun, and his courage. Allan's father had given it his whole life, and Allan simply must hang on until Bill Marley returned. He'd have to make do, have to stretch his resources, have to— A sudden, happy thought shone through his dark cloud of gloom.

He'd hoped to dazzle Tillotson with his big pike and he'd done so. But the encounter with Bob Torrance had stolen that moment of glory so completely that Allan hadn't given it one more thought. Now he remembered that his entry was almost sure to win the Spring Pike Derby. Its one hundred dollar prize, on top of a good season's earnings on his traplines, would see him through easily.

He beached his skiff in front of the house, saw Stormy up on the porch, and for a short space pointedly ignored the big dog. Told to stay at the house, Stormy was doing exactly that. But his ears were pricked up, his body was taut as a stretched rubber band, and his eager gaze was fixed on Allan. Relenting, Allan waved his hand.

"All right, Stormy."

Clearing the steps with one effortless leap, Stormy raced full speed forward. Always graceful despite his size, the big dog was never more so than when running. Allan had long since decided that his speed, as well as his size and grace, were a direct legacy from the wolf or staghound that showed so plainly. Reaching Allan, Stormy cavorted, pirouetted, and leaped playfully to snap his great jaws within a half-inch of Allan's shoulder.

As Allan ruffled the big dog's ears, hope sprang anew. He was not alone, but had a strong and loyal friend who'd help him no matter what he undertook. With Stormy beside him, he couldn't fail. This conviction stayed with him as he carried his pack into the house, stored the various articles it contained, and prepared the evening meal.

Darkness had not yet lowered when Stormy growled. Allan looked sharply at him. He was familiar with Stormy's bark and he'd heard his fighting snarl when he closed with a lynx. But this was a growl that told of danger to come.

"What is it?" Allan asked softly.

Stormy paced to the closed door and bristled, his attitude still one of complete alertness. Allan's heart plummeted to his toes.

Joe Torrance had told Allan that Bob had threatened to finish his fight, presumably as soon as he was sober enough to do so. Allan wanted no fights, yet he had to see. He opened the door slowly, in order to make as little noise as possible, then went through it swiftly. Stormy beside him, he ran around to the back of the house. Seeing and hearing nothing, he looked at Stormy.

The big dog stood tensely, reading the wind that blew from the lake. When Allan circled into the woods, Stormy followed, and did not leave Allan's side as he went cautiously forward. Slinking behind a tree, Allan peered around its trunk toward the lake shore.

Slap Happy Jackie, a .22 rifle in his hands, was peering earnestly at the place where Allan beached his skiff. Quietly as he had advanced, Allan retreated. There was no telling why Slap Happy Jackie had visited the lake, or why he should be carrying a gun when all hunting seasons were closed. However, Stormy was still technically an outlaw, and it was possible that Jackie would recognize him if he saw him. At any rate, Allan didn't think Jackie would touch the skiff. Circling back through the woods, Allan took Stormy into the house, closed the door, blew out the lights, and went to bed.

The next morning Allan got a spade from his tool shed and started working in his vegetable garden. It was an important spring duty, for he could always grow enough vegetables for summer use as well as many to store for winter. The garden did not pay off in cash, but what it did produce Allan would not have to buy.

Stormy watched politely for five minutes, but he had no lasting interest in spading. Released from guard duty and again free to live a dog's life, Stormy sniffed here and there and chased a couple of red squirrels. Finally, while Allan continued to toil, he lay blissfully down in the shade and went to sleep.

All that day and all the next morning Allan spaded, pulverized the few hard chunks he found, and sifted out and piled to one side the corn stubble and cabbage stalks from last year. After lunch he exchanged his jeans for an old and tattered pair and replaced his shoes with older ones. Then he took a spear from a closet, and screwed the various sections of wood handle into it.

Allan hefted the spear, a light and well-balanced instrument that was the best Johnny Malaming had been able to order for him. He turned it minutely to examine the point of each of the four prongs. Satisfied, he got a gunny sack from which the top third had been cut and to which he had attached straps so that it could be worn on the shoulder. Finally he went down to the lake, launched his skiff, laid spear and sack in the bottom, waited for Stormy to get aboard, and struck toward a bay on the lake's north shore. A cold little wind was kicking up a gentle swell, with now and then a white-capped wave.

Approaching the opposite shore, Allan stopped paddling to watch a hen mallard fussily shepherd her brood of ducklings toward some overhanging brush. The mallard and her family disappeared as though the brush had swallowed them, but Allan knew that they were merely lurking beneath it, and holding very still until he should pass. Allan smiled and went on. Occupied with trying to catch the giant pike, he'd had little time for a thorough springtime exploration of the lake. But present signs indicated that all was normal, with the usual complement of nesting waterfowl. Allan nosed into the bay for which he'd been heading and shipped his paddle.

An offshoot of the lake and with no cold springs of

its own, the shallow bay received the sun's direct rays all day long. Thus in summer it was always at least ten degrees warmer than the lake and showed it in vegetation which was much further advanced than any that grew in colder water. Rank cattails formed a thick hedge clear around the bay. Beyond them, in a swampy area three times the size of the bay itself, flat-leaved lily pads formed a green carpet so thick that it seemed to offer a solid footing. Wild rice grew among the lily pads and at scattered areas in the bay, and Allan examined one of the patches with keen approval. Seldom had he seen growth as lush. Wild rice was a favorite food of wild geese, and there should be geese in plenty this fall.

For five minutes Allan sat perfectly still. Then, in the lily pads beyond the hedge of cattails, he heard a loud splash. There was a little silence and another splash, then a half-dozen at once. Pushing through the marsh, Allan beached his skiff and climbed the little knoll against which he'd landed. He looked out on the lily pads.

Now they were not, as when seen from their own level, a solid covering. Broad leaves, attached to stems rooted in various depths of water, merely formed a mass that looked solid. Here and there was a quiet still pool from whose deeper waters the lily pads had not yet emerged. Nearer shore was a scattering of tussocks and patches of smaller pickerel-weed. There, only about ten feet away, Allan saw a fish.

About two feet long, and thick-bodied, the fish was having difficulty going through water too shallow to permit free passage for anything so bulky. Its scaled, bronzed back broke the surface, and the fish wriggled over a mud bar. At once it came back to roll sluggishly to and fro. All about other fish were similarly occupied. They had left the bay to spawn in this weed-choked marsh where the water was shallow and warm.

They were carp, no natives of North America but aliens from Europe that some optimist had imported to see if they'd do well. His wildest hopes had been exceeded; the carp had done so well that in places they'd already crowded out the native fish and had even found their way into remote lakes like this. Allan didn't know how they'd come here; perhaps there was a subterranean channel, or possibly a spring freshet had washed them into the upper reaches of Balsam Creek from some other pond or lake. But here they were, spawning again.

Allan looped the gunny sack's shoulder strap on his right shoulder and, spear in hand, leaped from the knoll to a tussock beneath it. Stormy, who approved of this wholeheartedly, splashed in beside him. Allan leaped from the tussock and waded toward the first carp he had seen. When he was close enough he thrust with his spear, transfixed the fish, and halted only long enough to transfer the carp from his spear to the gunny sack.

Immediately he was running after another carp, but slipped from a tussock and sprawled headlong in the swamp. Rising, he snatched up his spear, raced on, and made another easy catch. The hundreds of carp were so intent on the all-important business of spawning that they had little thought for any danger.

Allan filled his sack, dumped it into the skiff, and returned for another sackful. Not exactly a fish hunter but enjoying himself hugely, Stormy had a fine time chasing carp. Thoroughly soaked and coated with mud, he grinned in dog fashion at Allan.

"If you aren't an unholy mess!" Allan told him. "But I guess I don't look any better!"

When the skiff had all it could carry, Allan launched it and waited for Stormy to board. The big dog sprang into his accustomed place and promptly bounded right out again as slimy carp rolled beneath him. A skiff loaded with fish was not his idea of the proper place to ride.

Allan grinned, sent the skiff out into the bay, and watched Stormy paddle strongly in his wake. Allan picked up speed. He'd often wondered how fast a dog that was almost as much at home in water as on land could swim, and here was a chance to find out. Allan dipped his paddle deeply and the skiff spurted ahead.

Stormy hung back, not through any inability to swim faster but because he wanted to figure out what Allan was up to. Then he started to close in and had no trouble staying as near as he wished. Finally, entering wholeheartedly into the spirit of the thing, he surged ahead, swam clear around the skiff, and took up his place at the rear.

Allan laughed. With an unloaded skiff and a favorable wind pushing him, he might be able to leave Stormy behind. On the other hand, he might not.

Stormy hadn't had to call on all his speed in order to swim around the skiff.

When they reached the landing, Stormy climbed out, shook himself prodigiously, and sent spray flying in all directions. Then he halted with one forepaw uplifted. His head was up as he analyzed some elusive thread of scent that the wind brought him. Slowly at first and then more confidently, he went to a west window of the cabin and bent his head as he snuffled at something there. Allan followed and looked down at the plainly imprinted tracks of a man who had stood beside the window.

Allan pursed his lips thoughtfully. Someone had come visiting while he and Stormy were in the carp slough. Since there were no other boats on the lake, he must have followed the path that led from the freeway around the end of the lake. There was no good reason why someone shouldn't visit if he saw fit, but if he wanted to see Allan why hadn't he waited? Had he seen Stormy in the skiff and recognized him? Was it one of the Torrances, or Slap Happy Jackie, or someone else? He remembered the theft of the weasel pelts early last winter.

Allan stifled his curiosity. Jumping at conclusions, especially wrong conclusions, was one certain way to start trouble. Probably some wandering tourist, out for a hike, had simply stumbled across his house and wanted to see what it was like inside.

Allan shrugged, filled his gunny sack with carp, carried them to the garden, and buried them at strategic intervals. Fertilizer was expensive. But by utilizing the old Indian trick of burying fish in the garden, the Marleys had always had vegetables that equalled anyone else's.

Darkness had fallen before Allan buried the last carp. He was tired, but he'd done a good day's work. Tomorrow was visiting day at Laceyville and he'd have something encouraging to tell his father.

The late August sun was turning the water into a myriad of sparkling jewels as Allan paddled his skiff across a little pond far back in the Beaver Flowage. Cattails ringed the pond and wild rice almost choked it. On the shore, a doe with a spotted fawn beside her left her drinking place and stole quietly away. Wild ducks herded their now-feathered young into places of concealment. An osprey winged overhead. Few people even knew about this pond. For all practical purposes it was wild as it had been since long before Allan's grandfather first came upon it.

Allan worked a slow way around the pond, studying the bank as he did so. Muskrat trails were everywhere and the domed tops of their stick-and-mud houses broke the pond's surface in sixteen different places. Undoubtedly there were many additional muskrats that had chosen to burrow into the bank rather than build houses.

Satisfied, Allan beached his skiff. When spring came once more to the Beaver Flowage, a visit to this pond would more than pay off in fur. Allan shouldered the pack that lay in the skiff, balanced the skiff on top of it, and climbed a hardwood ridge to the next pond.

He put the skiff down gently, collected driftwood

that had floated ashore, built a fire, and while it blazed, cut a willow pole. Taking a hook and line from a tin box in his pocket, he tied the line to his pole, overturned rocks in wet earth beside the pond, and grabbed a few worms. He baited, cast, and yanked out one fat bluegill after another. While they were cooking, he delved into his pack to supplement the repast with cold beans and biscuits. He divided the meal with Stormy.

After they had eaten, they sat close beside the skiff, from which the fire reflected welcome warmth, and watched night close in. Summer was drawing to an end. Allan had tended his garden. With Stormy at his side he had prospected for new fur pockets, fished, studied the various waterfowl nesting in the Beaver Flowage, and merely explored for the fun of it. It was one of the most satisfactory summers Allan remembered. He had won the Pike Derby, and the prize money was in his tin box. No one had bothered him, and if his father had just been free to share the life they both loved, it would have been perfect.

The breeze, that all day long had blown steadily from the west, shifted abruptly to the north with nightfall, and became perceptibly colder. It hinted of frost, snow, sleet, and ice to come. Allan threw more wood on the fire, pillowed his head against Stormy, and gave himself to happy dreams. He did not fear the winter, and the night breeze spoke also of hordes of ducks that even now were gathering in flocks and discussing in their own fashion the long journey south. Waterfowl season, by far the finest time of the year, was just ahead.

9. Duck Season

Stormy stretched out beside him, Allan sat on the lake shore where he had an unobstructed view. Balanced across his knees was his twelve-gauge pump gun, its magazine plugged to permit insertion of only three shells. His canvas shooting jacket hung open. He wore no cap and little beads of sweat glistened on his forehead.

Waterfowl season had indeed arrived, but though it was on schedule according to the calendar, whoever decreed the official opening day had failed to supply the usual weather. The last days of August had been cool, and there'd been light frosts on both the first and second of September. Then had come a succession of days to rival any in June.

True, the Beaver Flowage had changed, with sumac and red maple blazing through their day of glory and other hardwoods turning color as they reached the proper stage. As though knowing they'd soon be ice-locked, muskrats sought still-succulent bulbs and roots and indulged in a very orgy of eating that almost approached gluttony. The fringed gentian, last wildflower to bloom, had uncovered its blue-purple flowers and faded. The signs of autumn were here, but most waterfowl still lingered in the north.

Allan tilted his head to the sky. There wasn't a cloud and the sun was both warm and summer-bright. But it was like a stage curtain meant to lull an audience while scenes of violence and terror were made ready behind it. This sort of weather would bear watching.

Lowering his head, Allan studied a little group of mallards that floated perhaps a quarter-mile from shore. He recognized the family. The duck had hatched a brood of ten in some rushes on the east side of the lake and brought all except two of her family safely through the summer. The drake had left what he probably considered unimportant details of family rearing to his wife and gone off by himself for the summer moult. Lately he had rejoined his mate and offspring, and now sported his autumn dress, not quite as bright as his winter plumage would be but almost so. Except that they were darker, the young were exact copies of their elders.

Stormy was watching the ducks too. Allan glanced at him, puzzled. When Stormy had seen the wing-tipped drake out on the ice, the big dog had immediately made it his business to retrieve it. Since then he'd seen many ducks without so much as chasing even one. It followed that he could distinguish between ducks that could fly and those that could not, and Allan wished he knew how the dog did it.

Allan looked back at the duck family, placidly paddling about. At such a distance, as they seemed well aware, the ducks were beyond shotgun range. As long as they were in open water, no unseen enemy could get near. It was not difficult to imagine why the experienced parents knew so much, but how did the young understand? Possibly they were merely following the example set by their elders. Beyond doubt, as soon as darkness provided safety, they'd all come to feed in the shallows. However, though mallards are one of the largest ducks and wonderful table fare, Allan had no interest in hunting these. They were "home" ducks that had nested on his lake. During the summer he'd come to know them, and he did not shoot his friends.

Far off, a shotgun boomed. Then a second hunter shot or the first one fired again. Allan listened indifferently. The only flight ducks he'd seen were a flock of blue-winged teal and a few pintails, both weather-sensitive species that are usually the first to fly south in the fall. Probably ninety per cent of the shooting enjoyed by hunters so far had been furnished by local birds. On the season's opening day, with a fair amount of unsophisticated young birds available, shotguns had boomed constantly. As the ducks became wary, shooting became sporadic and now only occasional shots were heard. Most of the early hunters had gone home. Though the economic status of Beaver Flowage waterfowl made no difference to him, Allan thought bitterly, he did worry about some of his friends who depended on hunters for a substantial portion of their income. Well, nobody would be left destitute. The weather would change and send the flights down soon, and more hunters would come—but not to his lake.

Allan rose. Shotgun in the crook of his arm, Stormy keeping pace, he started around the lake. The flights would come because they always came. When they did, he could get his quota of ducks and geese in no more than four days, or five at the most. But he could not forget that he hadn't even a penny to waste, therefore there were self-imposed restrictions. Blue-winged teal were fast and sporting, but they were also very small and Allan wanted more table fare than they provided for every shotgun shell expended. Pintails were big enough to be acceptable, but so far he had been unable to come within shotgun range of such as had arrived.

Searching the sky constantly, Allan tried to suppress the eagerness that throbbed within him. He thought Stormy a retriever second to none, but his only basis for that decision was the big dog's retrieve of the wing-tipped mallard last winter. Allan yearned to try Stormy over a shotgun and see what he could do then.

Suddenly, in the north and fairly high in the air, a V-wedge of black dots appeared. Allan ducked into the withered cattails, ordered Stormy down beside him, and raised his head just far enough to see the rapidly approaching ducks. Almost surely they were flight birds, but they were still out of shotgun range when Allan sighed and rose. The ducks were redheads, as their manner of flight indicated. They were big enough to be worth a shell and superior even to the famed canvasback as a table delicacy, some people claimed. But redheads nested well within territory that civilization claimed for its own. As a consequence, with many of their breeding and feeding marshes drained, their numbers had decreased more than that of any other duck with the exception of the extinct Labrador. Though he might have taken at least one, Allan chose to let all escape.

The ducks saw him when he rose, banked sharply, and beat back toward the other side of the lake. Allan ruffled Stormy's ears with his free hand.

"We'll strike oil yet, dog. Don't give up."

But it was mid-afternoon before another V-wedge of dots in the northern sky sent Allan dodging into the reeds and Stormy down beside him. As before, Allan kept very still and held his head just high enough so he could look between spaces in the reeds.

There were thirteen ducks and their line formation, slender red necks and white bodies, and driving speed marked them unmistakably as canvasbacks. It was strange that they should be here at all, for canvasbacks, one of the latest migrants, are so enamoured of the north and so reluctant to seek balmy southern weather that they often linger in the north until all ponds are frozen. But here they were, and as he watched them set their wings and come in for a landing, Allan's heart began to pound with the old familiar excitement. He marked down the reeds in which they landed and began his stalk.

Most waterfowl hunters prefer to shoot from blinds, a perfectly legitimate and sporting way to hunt. But partly because he enjoyed the thrill of the chase, and partly because it gave the ducks a better chance, Allan preferred to jump shoot. It was by no means a sure method of bagging any ducks, or even getting any shooting. Often Allan worked hours for one or two shots when, had he been in a blind, he might have had his choice of a dozen. But he still preferred jump shooting.

Rising, but stooping so that the brown back of his shooting jacket remained well below the tops of the reeds, he started slowly toward the sedges in which the canvasbacks had alighted. Utmost caution was imperative. An alien sound or sight would surely send them beating back into the air, hopelessly out of range. Glancing down at Stormy, Allan was astonished to see him walking as though he were treading on eggs. Obviously he had seen the canvasbacks descend. If he did not know they could be frightened, he would not now be trying so hard to avoid making noise. But how did he know the hunt was on? Or didn't he?

The flock of canvasbacks had alighted about four hundred yards away, and Allan took half an hour getting near enough to shoot. Then, gun ready to swing into position and right thumb on the safety catch, he stood erect. For a moment nothing happened. Then, with a little splashing and a quivering of the sedges among which they'd landed, the flock took to the air. As the ducks swung away, Allan sighted on a big drake and squeezed the trigger. As though he had suddenly collided with an invisible wall, the big drake tumbled toward the water. Allan sighted on a second duck, shot, and hastily pumped his third shell into the chamber. But by the time he raised his shotgun again the remaining ducks were out of effective range.

Meantime, Stormy had been leaping high to see

over the reeds. He leaped again and again, trying to keep the ducks in sight.

Allan slipped the safety back on, muttering to himself. The big drake, a clean kill, floated quietly where it had fallen. But the second duck at which he'd shot, and obviously wounded, already trailed the fleeing flock by at least twenty yards and was rapidly falling farther behind. As the flock went on, the wounded duck planed to the water two-thirds of the way across the bay from which the flock had taken flight.

Allan gritted his teeth; he hated to cripple ducks and have them die a lingering death. The flock had been well within range for both shots, so he had not violated his own code of ethics. But nobody who hunts ducks consistently can invariably score clean kills and must wound some. A trained retriever can find most cripples, but canvasbacks are in a class by themselves. Diving ducks, they often find their food in thirty feet of water. Wounded canvasbacks can dive to such depths, then swim long distances under water. There is never any way of knowing where they'll surface; they may come up for air in any quarter. Consequently, wounded canvasbacks are far and away one of the most difficult ducks to retrieve; Allan had heard experienced hunters say that it's impossible to retrieve one that can still swim.

Nevertheless, he had to try. He turned, intending to order Stormy to fetch the dead drake, but the dog was already surging through the rushes. He leaped from the top of a knoll, and landed with a mighty splash. He swam to the dead drake, got it, returned, and put it in Allan's hand. Wanting neither praise nor orders, he leaped away to get the other one.

The wounded duck, swimming, was so far out that it showed as little more than a white dot. Swimming with head and fore quarters as far out of water as he could keep them, the better to see, Stormy struck directly toward it. Allan estimated that the big dog was about fifty yards away from the duck when it dived.

Stormy treaded water, looking about. Then he raised his front quarters as high as he could, made a complete circle, and struck off at a thirty-degree angle to the course he had been following. Turning his eyes in this new direction, Allan saw the duck. Though it was impossible to judge distance with any accuracy under such circumstances, he thought that the wounded duck had surfaced much farther from the dog than it had been when it dived. Allan looked back at Stormy.

Seemingly confident, the big dog surged swiftly forward. Again, long before he was in a position to seize his quarry, the duck dived. Stormy repeated his previous maneuver of rising as high as possible in the water and turning clear around. He did it again, then struck off in a new direction.

Six times the duck surfaced. Six times, when Stormy passed what the canvasback evidently considered its safety margin, it dived. But with the sixth submersion, Stormy changed tactics. Rather than wait, rise in the water, and look all around to see where the duck surfaced, he set out on a long course that took him parallel to the opposite shore of the bay. When the canvasback finally surfaced, it did so no more than twenty feet or so from the swimming dog. Of course it was luck, Allan figured; Stormy couldn't possibly have known where his quarry would appear. A split second after it rose, the duck dived again.

Stormy resumed his patrol parallel to the opposite shore. Again the duck appeared. This time the dog's luck was against him for, while he was on the upbay side of his beat, the canvasback appeared on the down. Stormy swam straight toward it until it dived and took up his patrol again.

Allan thought he saw a definite pattern emerging from the dog's maneuvers. Every time the duck appeared, it was a little nearer the opposite shore and it began to look as though that was Stormy's sole objective. But wherein lay the advantage?

There were three more dives and surfacings, with the duck nearer the far shore every time. The wounded canvasback entered a shallow little cove on the far shore and dived again. Stormy swam into the cove and submerged. But when he came up, the wounded duck was in his jaws.

Stormy came straight back to Allan, climbed the knoll, and ceremoniously deposited the canvasback in his master's hand.

Allan's feet remained on the ground, but his heart soared higher than a wild goose. He had a duck dog! Stormy was not merely as good as any other retriever Allan had ever seen, but better. He'd chased his quarry until he understood its tactics. Then, with superb finesse, he had simply out-generaled it. Allan didn't know and never would know what had happened underwater in the little cove. He'd heard that some diving ducks, wounded and closely pursued, dive and take firm hold on a reed or stick that will keep them from surfacing. Perhaps this duck had finally resorted to such a maneuver and perhaps it hadn't. But regardless of what had taken place, Stormy had achieved the near-impossible; he had retrieved a wounded canvasback.

Stormy beside him, and still walking on air, Allan started toward home with his two ducks. He was still a considerable distance away when Stormy bristled and growled. Allan hesitated. On one previous occasion, when Slap Happy Jackie had prowled around Allan's boat landing, Stormy had acted in a similar fashion. There must be someone at or near the house.

Keeping Stormy close beside him, Allan swerved from the path into a grove of trees. He came to where he could see the house, peered around a tree trunk, and sighed in relief. Johnny Malaming sat on his porch. Allan stepped from behind the tree and approached openly.

"Hi, Johnny. What's with you?"

Johnny's eyes were on Stormy. "I know now why you was so all-fired interested in Jake Zermeich. Did you have that dog then?"

"Oh, I—" Allan tried to cover his confusion. "This dog?"

"That dog, the one that chawed Jake Zermeich."

"Are you sure, Johnny?"

"Yes, and so are you, but you needn't worry. The dog's no business of mine, and he acts all right. That ain't why I'm here. There's a couple of other things you should know."

"So?"

"Slap Happy Jackie's been shootin' off his trap. I can't figure his angle, but he don't like you and he keeps talkin' about this trouble between you and Bob Torrance."

Allan laughed. "I haven't seen Bob all summer, and if Jackie comes, I'll sick a catfish on him."

"Jackie ain't such a much," Johnny conceded, "but Bob Torrance's back in town. He's roarin' drunk and tellin' everybody that this time he aims to clean your clock for what your pa did to his."

"He was going to do the same last spring."

"Joe fixed that up. Soon's Bob was sober enough, Joe saw that he left. But Joe won't stop him now; he's spoilin' for trouble."

There was an awkward silence. Johnny broke it by getting to his feet.

"Thought you'd like to know."

"Thanks. Thanks a lot, Johnny. There won't be any trouble with Bob."

Johnny descended the steps, and without a word or backward look started toward the Tillotson freeway.

"Johnny!" Allan called. "You won't tell about my dog?"

Johnny stopped and turned. "Time I get to Tillotson I won't even remember you got a dog, if that's what you want. The only thing I wish is that he'd chawed Jake Zermeich some more while he was at it."

Two days later, Allan had prepared an early evening meal, fed Stormy, and was washing the dishes
when Stormy growled again. A minute later came a
knock at the door and the sound of a familiar voice.

Allan opened the door to admit Jeff Darnley, the
game warden.

10. Under Suspicion

As befitted the weather, the little warden was dressed in ordinary walking shoes, summer-weight shirt and trousers, a light sweater with only the lower button fastened, and an old brown hat pushed back on his head. There was a smile on his lips, but his eyes were hard and unreadable.

"Hello, Jeff," Allan greeted him. "Come on in."

Still bristled, Stormy walked to the far wall and lay down where he could watch this stranger. Jeff looked at him, then turned accusing eyes on Allan.

"Didn't you tell me you hadn't seen that dog?"

"I said I hadn't seen a killer dog," Allan corrected. "I *know* he isn't. But he's just about the smoothest and smartest retriever you ever saw."

"He is, eh? How long have you had him?"

"He came here last November. First time I saw him, he was going out on the ice to get a wing-tipped mallard. That was the one I brought you. Remember?"

Jeff snorted. "I remember right enough. I also remember that, while you were there, I asked about this dog. Did you know at the time that he'd pitched into a man named Zermeich?"

"Yes."

"And you still said nothing?"

"There wasn't anything wrong with him except that he'd been mistreated. Ask Johnny Malaming how this fellow Zermeich treats animals."

Jeff shrugged. "All right, Al. Nothing wrong about adopting a stray dog. As long as this one stays out of trouble he'll get none from me. But get a license for him. Anyhow, I came for a different reason. What do you know about Bob Torrance?"

Jeff's hard eyes seemed to burn into Allan's and Allan wondered. What did the warden expect him to do or say? What reaction was Jeff anticipating? There was more to his question than had yet appeared.

"Johnny Malaming said he was back and looking for trouble. I wish he'd let me alone. I don't bother him."

"*Has* there been any trouble?" Jeff asked sharply.

"Not since last spring," Allan said positively. "He tried to pick a fight with me in Johnny Malaming's store, just before I won the Pike Derby. I backed down. Then I saw Joe Torrance and he warned me that he'd come over and take me apart himself if I beat Bob up. Joe and his drunken brother!"

"That's all?"

"That's enough!" Allan flared. "Aren't the Torrances satisfied, with Dad in jail and Joe fixing the freeway so hunters don't come here any more?"

"I meant has there been any more trouble between you and Bob?"

"I haven't seen him since spring! I told you—"

"I know the background," Jeff said understand-

ingly, "and I know how hard it's been for you to keep
going here." He cleared his throat. "Get any ducks
today?"

"Two baldpates and a pintail. Why?"

"At this end of the lake?"

"No, in the north marsh. Say, what—"

Jeff laid a hand on his arm. "There's been some
serious trouble."

"What are you talking about?"

"I made a patrol on Gull Lake today," Jeff said
slowly. "Coming back, I cut cross-country and came
out at the foot of the freeway, near where you beach
your skiff."

"Go on," Allan said tensely.

"I found Bob Torrance there. He was dead, and as
nearly as I could determine, a .22 bullet in the head
killed him."

"Dead!" Allan gasped.

"Yes," the warden said quietly. "That's why I
came here."

"But—but I haven't even seen Bob!" Allan stam-
mered.

"I believe you, Al, and I've questioned too many
men not to know when they slip. But I did want to
see if I could make you tell me anything."

Allan's head reeled. Bob Torrance shot, lying dead
near the skiff landing that nobody but himself used!
And Bob had been telling everybody he was going to
finish his fight with Allan . . .

Jeff Darnley's eyes had softened, and he was looking sympathetically at Allan.

"Do you trust me?" the warden asked gently.

"Why, sure."

"Enough to put yourself in my hands?"

Allan remained too shaken to think clearly. "What do you have in mind?"

"I want to take you to Tillotson and put you up at my house. Somebody shot Bob, either accidentally or intentionally, and whoever did it will be found. When he is, it will be safe for you to come back here."

"I . . . I don't know."

"It's the wisest course," Jeff urged. "When the Torrances find out about Bob, they'll start looking for you."

"They'll think I shot him, you mean?"

"Beyond any doubt, and they'll act accordingly. There's trouble enough now, without asking for any more."

"They won't catch me."

"They won't if you do as I say."

"I—I can't do it, Jeff!"

"Why can't you?"

"Because I'd be a—a coward," Allan fumbled. "Besides, being cooped up in your house, afraid to go out, would be like—like being in jail." That wasn't what he meant; how could he explain? "Look, Jeff," he said desperately. "If I left here, I'd be leaving something that I've been fighting for, fighting for against the Torrances, and not having enough money, and no hunters, and no Dad. I've had furs stolen, and people snooping around, and threats and insults, but I've tried to keep my temper and mind my own business." He broke off and drew a deep breath. "I guess I'm like Stormy. There are some things I just can't take."

Jeff's eyes hadn't left Allan's face. "I know how you feel, but that's not the point. If the Torrances come boiling over here, and they're likely to, you'll be a sitting duck."

"No I won't. Stormy and I will be someplace where they'll never find us."

"Where?" the warden asked skeptically.

"Up Black Creek."

Jeff's eyes widened. "Where's that?"

"See!" Allan said triumphantly. "*You* don't even know. It's a branch of Balsam Creek that flows in through a marsh. It's got about ten channels, and only Dad and I know how to follow the main one."

While he was talking, Allan dragged out his pack basket and began to load it.

"Wait a minute!" Jeff told him. "I'm convinced you didn't shoot Bob Torrance, but this business is up to the sheriff, not me. If you take off in this hare-brained way, it'll look as if—"

"You'll know where I am," Allan assured him, "and that I'm not a fugitive. When you want me, go up Balsam Creek to a fork by a big, dead sycamore. Take the left fork until you come to a marsh. Fire three shots and I'll come to you. I promise I will."

The warden had been staring at the floor, thinking. "All right, kid," he said reluctantly. "You've had a tough time and I guess I can do this much for you. Now I've got to phone the sheriff." He glanced out the window. "It's almost dark now, so nobody will see you leave. I'll be up Balsam Creek in three days, with whatever news there is. Good luck."

"Thanks, Jeff," Allan said feelingly.

As soon as the door had closed behind the warden, Allan rechecked the contents of his pack basket. He tried to force himself to think clearly, for he must remember everything he should carry with him. There'd be no coming back for any forgotten article. Mindful of the veiled threat behind the blue skies of the past few days, he packed his rubber-bottomed pacs, wool clothing, and mittens. He topped the load with a box of shotgun shells. Ducks would supplement his food, and with shotguns booming all over the Beaver Flowage, his wouldn't even be noticed. Finally he strapped on the belt that held his hatchet and .22 revolver, picked up his shotgun, and turned to Stormy.

"Come on, dog," he said sharply. "We're going camping."

Stormy close behind, Allan went down the path to the lake. He launched his skiff, waited for Stormy to get in, and started out in the gathering dusk. He had nearly reached the mouth of Balsam Creek, and complete darkness had fallen, when he remembered the tin box of money under the floor. He wouldn't need it where he was going, but suppose whoever had come prowling before should see the house deserted for a couple of days and really ransack it?

Turning the skiff, he started back, setting his course across the dark water by the first faint stars.

He was halfway past the larger island when he saw flashlights bobbing on the porch and a light come on in the house.

The Torrances had come.

11. The Watcher

In the dim light of very early morning, Allan awakened beneath a big, dead sycamore. Looking down at the remains of the little fire beside which he'd slept, he kicked the ashes and charred stubs into the water. He launched his skiff, let Stormy aboard, and started up a creek so narrow that he might have touched either bank with his paddle. It was so thickly bordered with bushy hemlocks that, in the weak light, it was almost suggestive of a jungle stream. Presently the thick little hemlocks gave way to withered rushes and cattails. Beyond them a marsh opened out, cut by a wandering stream that at intervals separated into anywhere from three to as many as twelve channels. This was Black Creek, where all the channels except one ended blindly in some bog. Allan and his father had worked the maze out while trapping muskrats in the marsh.

Allan swerved into a side channel and a little flock of blue-winged teal scudded to the bank and hid in the thick growth. Stormy pricked up interested ears and glanced back at his master. Then he looked hopefully at the shotgun. When Allan made no move to pick it up, Stormy flattened his ears and resigned himself to no hunting for the present.

There was not the faintest suggestion of a breeze,

and rather than the hoar frost that should have been evident at this hour and season, only a light mist could be seen. Allan paddled to the bank and beached his skiff. Stormy leaped out, climbed a little way up the bank, and waited expectantly. Pulling his skiff up far enough so that no sudden wind could set it adrift, Allan probed into the pack basket for food.

The day lightened slowly but steadily. Presently the sun, a lemon-colored ball, appeared over the eastern horizon and lingered as though reluctant to climb higher. Allan glanced at it and thought that when the weather broke there would be a violent eruption. The sun's color indicated little dust in the air, as if the whole land was a vacuum just waiting for a storm to roar into it.

Allan wasn't hungry enough to build another fire and cook breakfast. He opened a can of dog food for Stormy, and for himself just spread cold beans on a slice of bread, clapped another slice on top of it, and ate. Finishing only half his sandwich, he gave the rest to Stormy and lost himself in thought. Yesterday's events, not to mention the future, needed some serious consideration.

He did not doubt Jeff Darnley, or question that Jeff had anything except Allan's own best interests at heart in wishing to keep him out of the way of the Torrances. Nor was there any question that the Torrances were in an ugly mood last night and would have dealt with him in a summary fashion if he'd been home. Who could prove otherwise if half a dozen men swore that Allan had opened fire when they came and they'd been forced to shoot back in self defense? Well, he hadn't been there, and even if they'd had boats, the Torrances wouldn't have been able to catch him in the dark. And they'd never find him here.

However, where did that leave him? Everyone knew that Bob Torrance had been after him, and now Bob had been found shot dead at Allan's skiff landing. That would be enough for most people.

Jeff had told him that the guilty party would surely be found; that would automatically clear Allan. But supposing the guilty party wasn't found? More than one shooting "accident" remained unsolved, and the more Allan considered it, the more damning seemed the evidence against him. Had he done the right thing in insisting on staying out here? He had food enough for a few days, but if Bob's slayer weren't found, he'd have to go away. Transportation cost money, and his money was back home in a tin box under the floor. Could he still get it?

Allan considered. In this hiding place on Black Creek, he knew that he was safe from discovery. On the other hand, he didn't know what was going on at the lake. If he took the skiff back through the marsh and down Balsam Creek, he might run into somebody. But he could also get back to the lake over land. Black Creek ran generally south from Balsam Creek, and if he continued south on foot from where he was, he would soon come out on the lake shore within sight of his house. If nobody was around . . .

The sun was high in the sky, and its rays fell full strength on the back of Allan's shooting jacket as he wriggled through the withered reeds. He shrugged out of the jacket and left it. Before going on, he paused to watch a small flight of ducks speed over the lake and dip down to it. At first he thought they were mallards, but as they braked to land, their yellow feet identified them as gadwalls.

Stormy, whose back remained well below the reeds, kept pace with his wriggling master until Allan saw the glint of water ahead. He put a restraining hand on Stormy's ruff and the big dog halted at once.

"Down!" Allan commanded.

Stormy lay down, and Allan crawled forward to the edge of the lake. He parted the reeds with his hand and looked out.

He was on the shore opposite his home. About three hundred yards from shore and to Allan's right was the larger of the lake's two islands, marked by its single tall aspen. After a brief glance, and seeing no one, Allan looked across at his house. A plume of blue smoke curled from the chimney; smoke meant that somebody was occupying the place. His heart sank. Evidently the Torrances hadn't overlooked the possibility that Allan might try to return, and had left a guard.

Presently a man emerged from the house and came down to the lake. He was of average size, and too far away for his features to be distinguished. Allan muttered under his breath. His packing, which last night had seemed so thorough, had indeed been slipshod. He had not only forgotten his money, but a good pair of binoculars he owned. The man whiled away his time by tossing pebbles into the water.

Ten minutes later, faint in the distance, Allan heard the rumble of a truck. Presently, at the foot of the freeway, the truck appeared and stopped. Men jumped from the cab and body and busied themselves unloading the vehicle. Allan strained to see what they were doing. They were lifting boats from the truck and launching them. Allan counted three. Two men set out in the first, and Allan tried to identify them, but they were too far away. Each manned by two men, the other boats set out.

Then a man carrying a canoe came down to the lake shore. He launched his trim craft, took the rear seat, and another man got in front. Allan's glance darted back to the boats, that were spreading out to head for various portions of the lake. They were a far cry from the lumbering craft which are usually rented to tourists, and their crews seemed to know how to get the best out of them. But graceful though they were, the boats still seemed awkward compared to the canoe or to Allan's skiff.

Allan tried to identify the canoemen, heading straight down the lake, but they passed too far away. Then a boat headed toward Allan's side of the lake and cut at right angles when less than fifty feet from shore. It passed so close that Allan might have cast a stone into it, and he had no difficulty recognizing the boatmen. They were Ballard Torrance and Jack Hardy, a Torrance cousin. Evidently the clan was out in force. Furthermore, Allan thought bitterly, Joe

Torrance had opened the freeway for the first time in two seasons—to look for him. He began to wriggle back through the reeds. Today was a lost cause; he'd come back for another look tomorrow.

For the first time in nearly three weeks, the sky was bridged with a surging bank of clouds whose color ranged from dull black to pure white. A brisk wind kicked up whitecapped waves. His light hunting jacket and trousers discarded in favor of heavier wool clothing, Allan crept toward his vantage point, Stormy beside him. Telling the dog to stay, Allan parted the reeds and looked across the lake.

Since yesterday morning, the waterfowl population had increased a hundredfold. Ducks and geese had come winging out of the north, anxious migrants that had at last recognized the inevitability of winter and knew they must flee. The blue-winged teal, pintails, and other early migrants, as well as the majority of the home ducks, had taken wing and gone farther south. But their absence was unnoticeable now.

A flock of at least two hundred and fifty mallards, with which mingled about half that many of their first cousins, the black ducks, rode the whitecaps a safe distance from shore. A number of baldpates, that left their nesting ground early enough but were inclined to loiter on the way south, lingered near the mallards and black ducks. There was even a flock of green-winged teal, that are not quite so sensitive to cold as their blue-winged relatives. About a hundred Canada Geese kept haughtily aloof in the lake's center, and though most slept with heads tucked beneath wings, at least five sentinels were constantly alert.

Warm weather, the great dam that had held all these migrants back, had finally burst and let the feathered horde spill southward. More flocks, numbering anywhere from three to as many as fifty birds, arrived so frequently that they seemed to be alighting every minute. Scattered on the lake were small flocks and individual birds too numerous to count.

Judging by the clouds, the first winter storm might break at any minute. But this was still only mid-October, too early for winter to clamp down and stay even though it might throw a few preliminary punches. There would be good waterfowl hunting for at least three weeks and possibly longer. But for the first time since he could remember Allan felt none of the tingling excitement which the great autumn migration had never before failed to inspire. The black pall hanging over him cast a shadow so dark and gloomy that there was room for nothing else, and he thought only that the arrival of so many flight birds certainly marked the end of summer.

As the day wore on, Allan kept his vigil. He saw men moving about his house, though he could not identify them. He saw the first rowboat return in mid-morning, to be followed in two hours by the second. Then the third beat its way across the tossing lake. Only the two canoemen had not yet returned. When they did, Allan would work his way back to his hideout and wait for Jeff Darnley to come tomorrow as he had promised.

Aroused by beating wings directly overhead,

Allan tilted his head. Flying in small flocks but many of them, the canvasbacks were arriving in force. They flew out over the lake, dipped, braked to a halt with their wings, and settled on the water. Allan studied them with great interest.

There had been a silent threat while the mild weather reigned, a promise of drastic change to come. That threat was becoming a reality by the arrival of so many ducks and geese, and clinched beyond possible doubt by the coming of the canvasbacks. Hunting pressure had never forced so many of them down. They were fleeing cold weather, bitter weather.

The wind strengthened, and waves that had been beating onto the big island now surged over the dead willows with which it was bordered. Pattering snow began to fall, faster and faster. The downfall gathered fury so fast that within minutes Allan could see the island only in outline and was unable to see the far shore at all. This had all the signs of a feared black storm.

Sweeping his gaze across the lake, Allan suddenly saw the canoe. It was halfway between the shore upon which Allan lay and the big island, and making desperately for the latter. Through thickening snow Allan made out Joe Torrance at the bow paddle and Jeff Darnley in the rear. He held his breath.

Straight out of the north, the wind was lashing the lake into waves as big as any Allan had ever seen. Given a choice, he'd never launch his skiff in such water and certainly it was no place for a canoe. Without even a faint chance of making the shore, the island was the canoemen's only hope and they'd be lucky to reach that. But they continued to handle their frail craft with consummate skill and were within a paddle stroke of safety when the canoe grounded on a rock or submerged log and turned sidewise. Waves hid canoe and canoemen in a smother of spray, while Allan stared. Presently, and dimly through the swirling sheets of snow, he saw one of the canoemen half-carrying and half-dragging the other up onto the island.

Calling Stormy, Allan fought his way back through the reeds and began to run toward his hidden skiff.

12. Black Storm

When he reached the spot where he had hidden the
skiff, Allan found that the concealing reeds, brown
and bare when he left this morning, were now cush-
ioned with snow. In spite of his great sense of
urgency, he forced himself to a measure of clear
thinking. The temperature was probably about fifteen or twenty above, dangerous to anyone who'd
been in the lake. Willow sticks offered the only ma-
terial on the island from which a fire might be built,
and they were next to useless as fuel. In addition,
one of the two men who'd landed there was hurt.
Warmth was the first consideration.

He upended his pack basket and spilled its contents into the snow. Empty basket in one hand and
hatchet in the other, he ran down the stream bank to
the nearest hemlocks. Using the blunt side of his
hatchet to smash the branches from a dead hemlock,
Allan broke them up and put them in the basket. He
took time to load the basket carefully, for it would
hold three times as much properly packed as it might
if sticks were thrown in haphazardly. The basket
finally filled, Allan shoved his hatchet into his belt
sheath and followed the stream back to his skiff,
bending his head as the wind struck him. In the half

hour or so that had elapsed since he left the lake shore, the storm had mounted to a savage pitch.

Allan stooped to upend the skiff over his head and it was almost blown from his hands. Allan clenched his jaw. There were two men in desperate trouble on the island and the only help they could possibly have must come from him. But he couldn't reach them without the skiff and obviously he couldn't carry it.

Stormy, his black coat sprinkled with white, shook himself, rolled happily in the snow, then shook himself again. That gave Allan an idea. He couldn't carry the skiff, but he could drag it over the soft snow. He grasped the anchor rope and started overland toward the lake.

The snow was falling so fast and the wind blowing it so furiously that the tracks he'd made were all but erased. Stooping forward, partly to shield himself from the storm and partly to see the faint tracks more clearly, Allan towed his skiff back toward the rushes where he'd lain to watch his house. When he got there, visibility was so limited that nothing more than a few feet away had a clear shape and form. But he could see the waves, all right; they seemed twice as high as they had been. Allan glanced toward the island and couldn't see it. He tried another quarter, and still another, then returned his gaze to where he knew the island must be. Very faintly against the sky, he saw the topmost branches of the tall aspen whipping furiously in the gale. There was still time but he must act fast.

He shoved the skiff into the water, then gripped

the anchor rope desperately as the wind tried to wrench the craft away from him. Working his hands down the anchor rope, Allan grasped and steadied the skiff.

"Get in, Stormy!" he shouted.

Unconcerned by wind and waves, Stormy waded out and jumped into his accustomed place. Paddle gripped for instant use, Allan seated himself and set out on the tossing lake. The skiff leaped ahead.

Although he couldn't see it, Allan knew that the island was to his right, about two hundred yards from shore. He guided himself by the feel of his skiff and the direction of the wind. The skiff mounted the crest of one wave, sank into the following trough, and a little water splashed over the bow. Allan gave a mighty forward stroke and at once dipped his paddle again. Doggedly he kept on, fighting the seas that surged against him and at times seemed to be coming from all directions at once. Was he losing ground, or was he gaining? He couldn't be sure.

At intervals he lifted his head to look for the island, and when he could not see it he began to worry. Just as he became convinced that he had miscalculated and should try another course, he saw the topmost branches of the aspen. Waiting his chance, he turned the skiff toward the island. The wind took over, so that all he had to do was dip his paddle enough to keep headed straight and let the wind push him. It gave him a chance to rest, and he gulped great breaths into his gasping lungs. He was ready when a wave rolled the skiff up onto the island.

As he leaped out, Allan noted mechanically that

Stormy had already jumped out and was awaiting him. Stooping, Allan dragged the skiff beyond reach of the battering waves, then looked about. He'd reached the island, and somewhere on it were two men in desperate need. But where? The snow had increased so that not even the willow branches around him had a clear outline.

"Hall-oo!" Allan called.

It was meant to be a mighty shout, but the wind snatched it from his lips and reduced it to a choked whisper. However, Stormy heard him, and shoved his nose against Allan's knee. That gave him an idea; a dog might succeed where a man would fail. Allan knelt and spoke in the big mongrel's ear.

"Where are they? Find them, Stormy!"

Stormy whined and lifted a front paw to his master's thigh. Allan's hopes sank. Stormy had never hunted men and there was no reason to suppose he'd know what Allan meant.

Pulling the skiff behind him, for if he lost it he probably couldn't find it again, Allan struck along the island's shore. It was a poor way to try to find the two castaways, by searching blindly, but it was the only way he had. When he stopped to rest, he noticed that Stormy was no longer with him. Allan felt a fleeting fear lest the dog be lost too, but the fear faded almost in the same second. Stormy just didn't get lost.

Presently the dog reappeared, ghostly in the snow, and looked back over his shoulder. Acting on sudden impulse, Allan started in the direction from which the dog had come. Stormy pacing a few feet ahead of

him, Allan dipped into a little swale and suddenly
found the men he was seeking.

His head pillowed on a rolled-up coat, and
shielded to some extent by a crude wall of snow, Jeff
Darnley lay full length and very still. Joe Torrance
huddled in the lee of a boulder, where scuffed snow
and a tiny pile of willow sticks bore pathetic tes-
timony to his efforts to build a fire. With shaking
fingers he was attempting to ignite his little pile of
sticks, but when he tried to strike the match it fell
into the snow.

Allan turned the skiff on its side as shelter from the
wind, kicked a hole in the snow, and emptied the
contents of his pack basket beside the skiff. He arranged small hemlock twigs, applied a lighted
match, watched flame climb through the twigs, and
added larger wood. As the fire leaped up, Allan stole
a glance at Joe Torrance.

So numb that he could barely move, Joe had riveted his eyes on the fire as if he had never seen one
before. It occurred to Allan, in a vague and unreal
way, that he and Joe hated each other. But the
thought was fleeting; it wasn't important now.

Stooping beside Jeff Darnley, Allan put one hand
around the little warden's shoulders and the other
beneath his knees. He carried Jeff close to the fire,
laid him down, and shifted the skiff to give as much
protection as possible from wind and blowing snow.
Unbuttoning the warden's sodden clothing, Allan
began vigorously to massage his cold flesh. The
stimulation, plus the fire's warmth, brought circula-
tion back to what had seemed a dead body. Lifting

and turning Jeff as he worked, Allan stripped him. Then he removed his own dry clothing, put it on Jeff, and struggled into the warden's much smaller garments.

"Wh—Wh—What . . ."

Joe Torrance was trying to speak, and Allan went over to him. He helped Joe up, and got him nearer the fire.

"What's wrong with Jeff?" Allan asked.

"Knee . . . twisted," Joe mumbled between numb lips. "C-c-can't walk."

"I'm going to take him in and come back for you!" Allan told him.

"Th-th-think you c-can make it?"

"I have to make it!"

Joe tried to get up, stumbled back, then tried a second time and made it. Allan took off the belt that held his hatchet and .22 revolver and buckled them around Joe.

"The cylinder's full and there are more cartridges in the belt," he said. "Wait an hour, then shoot three times! Repeat three shots every few minutes until I come back!"

Joe, massaging his hands over the fire, nodded his understanding.

"I'm going to pull the skiff to the other side of the island and launch it from there, with the wind!" Allan told him. "You wait here with Jeff. I'll come back for him when I get the skiff set."

"I'll bring Jeff," Joe offered.

"If you're able to, let's go!"

Allan pulled the skiff, breaking a path, and Stormy

padded beside him. Joe Torrance brought up the rear, the unconscious warden in his arms. There was no need to grope for direction, for the wind remained from the north and they had only to keep it at their backs in order to reach the island's lee side.

When they reached the lake, Allan turned to take Jeff Darnley. Sliding the warden's feet under the front seat, he rested Jeff's head in the bow.

"I'll leave Stormy with you," he told Joe.

"Stormy?"

"The dog! Start back to the fire now!"

Allan skidded the skiff forward, stepped into the paddler's seat just as it touched water, and a minute later was lost in the storm. He had to narrow his eyes against the driving snow. Even so, going over would be easy; all he had to do was keep the skiff straight and let the wind push it. But coming back . . .

Pushed by the wind, needing only an occasional dip of the paddle to keep it straight, the skiff seemed to fly rather than float toward the opposite shore. Once Allan thought he heard the gabbling of waterfowl, then decided that the only sound he could possibly hear was the wind.

Suddenly he saw waves breaking on shore and felt a momentary panic; he couldn't possibly have crossed the lake. Then he noted a knobby-branched sycamore that overhung the water and blessed his luck. He'd thought the wind would carry him to within a few hundred yards of his house, but this sycamore was less than a hundred feet west of the path leading to his front door.

Allan stepped out with the wave that carried the

skiff onto the beach, pulled it farther, and turned to gather Jeff Darnley in his arms. As he carried him up the beach, dimly through falling snow, Allan saw lighted windows. He struggled up the path, across the porch, and pushed the door open with his knee. There were several men inside and Allan shoved Jeff Darnley at the first one he saw. It was Ballard Torrance.

"He's hurt! Take care of him!" Allan told Ballard.

Immediately he turned and, leaving a babble of surprised voices behind him, raced back to the skiff. There was another man on the island. There was a dog too, and Allan was going back for them, in spite of the whole Torrance clan.

Allan turned the skiff around, and even as he slid it back toward the lake, he knew he was in trouble. It had been relatively easy to launch with the wind, but now it was against him, and great waves were rolling far up the beach. He tried to float his light craft on the first wave, and found himself six feet farther up the shore, in a sitting position, with the skiff across his lap and the wave bursting around him.

He tilted the skiff to spill the water out, then lifted it waist high. He waded straight into the next wave, and stood with braced feet as it rolled past him. Hurriedly he dropped his skiff in the trough, and though the little craft rocked dangerously when he boarded, it did not capsize. Allan snatched up his paddle, fighting the next wave that strove to hurl him back on shore. Then he was out on the lake.

Allan concentrated all his attention and strength on paddling. Coming over with Jeff, the wind squarely at his back, he had landed almost at his own front door. It stood to reason that, if he faced into the eye of the wind now, he must come again to the island, or at least within sound of Joe's signal shots. He was already tired, but he dared not rest, for to do so would mean that he'd be swept back all the distance he'd gained.

After a while he decided that the wind had veered from true north to ten or fifteen degrees northwest. But though he was tempted to alter his own course to compensate, Allan kept straight on. One wrong guess in a situation such as this would be one too many. But where were the shots that he should have been hearing before this?

He had been paddling for hours on end, it seemed, and was sure he had missed the island, when he thought he heard the snapping report of a .22. He veered toward the sound, heard it again, and a few minutes later saw the island. Allan swung to quarter around it; it would be hazardous to attempt a landing except on the lee side. When he felt the force of the wind slacken, Allan swung toward land.

He drew his skiff up, but could not tell exactly where he was. He shouted, but there was no answer. Straining to listen, Allan heard only the wind. He grasped the anchor rope and was on the point of setting out to look when Stormy bounded to his side. Allan knelt to hug the big dog, then rose to follow as Stormy returned to the boulder beside which Joe Torrance waited. The fire had burned itself into cold ashes.

"I got Jeff back," Allan panted. "Come on; skiff's this way!"

The wind at their backs, they started toward the island's lee shore. Following Allan's tracks, they came to the edge of the water and found the skiff.

"Take the bow," Allan told Joe.

Without question, Joe seated himself and Stormy jumped in. Allan shoved the skiff out, stepped in himself just as the stern floated, and hastily snatched up his paddle. Again the wind sent them skimming forward. Dipping his paddle just enough to maintain a straight course, Allan groaned with the sheer luxury of resting his tired body. The nightmare lay behind.

He was completely unprepared for the sudden, harsh grating of the skiff's bottom and the abrupt rising of the bow. Joe Torrance tumbled backward and Stormy skidded into him. From the storm-lashed waters rose a weird monster. It was only a floating dead tree on whose submerged trunk the skiff had grounded, but it acted alive. Rolling over, the tree brought its arm-like branches to the surface and one of them collided suddenly with Allan's head. The skiff turned over.

Allan realized that he was in the lake, but could think of nothing except that the water was warmer than the wind. Then he heard a frantic voice.

"Allan! Allan! Where are you?"

The voice partially brought him to. It sounded familiar, and instinctively he began to swim toward it. He felt a hand seize him, felt it lift his right arm and curl it around a dog's neck. Allan smiled bliss-fully. Stormy. He should have known that Stormy would stay with him, and that together they could do anything. Allan twined his fingers in the dog's fur and was dreamily aware of the fact that Stormy was swimming.

Then he felt shallows beneath his feet and tried to walk. He almost fell, managed to stay erect, and staggered toward the shore. Then he fell again and did not move.

Allan awoke to a sense of failure. He'd left Stormy and Joe Torrance on an island, he remembered, and they'd depended on him for rescue. But instead of going back for them, he'd taken time to rest. Allan struggled to a sitting position.

As soon as he did, he saw that he was in his own bed in his own house. Burning wood snapped cheer-fully, and the sides of his heating stove glowed cherry red. Sunlight streamed through the windows and the wind was no longer howling. Jeff Darnley and Joe Torrance were sitting by the stove, Jeff with one leg resting on another chair. Beside Allan's bed, Stormy was thumping his tail and watching him.

Allan ruffled the dog's ears. Suddenly weak, he sank back on his pillow and turned to the two men.

"What happened?"

"You were going great until we grounded on a dead tree," Joe Torrance said. "Then the skiff cap-sized. I floated in with it, but your dog towed you. That's some dog. Wish I had him."

Allan heard his own voice say, "You wouldn't want an outlaw!" Why had he said that?

"Outlaw?" Joe arched questioning brows at Jeff. "What's he mean?"

"Al's still a little delirious," Jeff said soothingly.

Allan's head began to clear and he sat up again, looking around the room. "Where are the rest?"

"They went home when the weather cleared."

"But—but—"

Joe's voice was low-pitched. "I know what you're thinkin', Al, and you're right. We were the biggest pack of fools in the Beaver Flowage. Slap Happy Jackie told us about Bob, and we came boilin' over here to—to— Aw, you tell him, Jeff."

The warden smiled grimly. "It was a near thing, Al. They did come after you. Slap Happy Jackie put them up to it, figuring that would take care of everything. Only he's not very bright; he knew more about Bob's shooting than he should."

Allan stared at him. "You mean Slap Happy—"

Jeff nodded. "He shot Bob. Whether it was an accident or not, only the trial can tell. Anyway, after he confessed, the Torrances realized what they'd done, or might have done—"

"That's why we brought boats to the lake," Joe put in eagerly. "We were tryin' to find you and explain."

Allan turned to Jeff. "But you knew where I was."

"I thought I did," the warden replied. "Joe and I took a canoe up Balsam Creek to the fork, like you said, and then up Black—"

"Oh," Allan said, red-faced. "I wasn't on Black

Creek then. I was watching across the lake. You said three days, and I thought—"

"There was a storm, remember?" Jeff pointed out wryly. "We were trying to get you out of there before it broke. Instead, you got us out. Thanks."

"Then I guess we're even," Allan fumbled, unable to take in the fact that he was no longer under suspicion.

"Not even enough to suit me," Joe said. "Look, Al, we had to open the freeway to truck in those boats. I—uh—suppose we left it open? It's kinda late this season, but next year, when the ducks are flyin' and your dad's back . . ."

Stormy had become bored with all the talk. He got to his feet and nudged Allan's hand for attention. Allan closed his fingers around the big black muzzle.

"Stormy's all for it," he said happily.

ABOUT THE AUTHOR

JIM KJELGAARD spent his boyhood in country much like that described in this book. "Those mountain farms," he remembers, "produced more rocks to the acre than anything else. But they provided my brothers and me with plenty of ammunition for fighting the neighboring boys across the creek. One of our jobs was to shoo the cows out of the corn patch, which was more exciting than it sounds. There were always two or three yearling bulls in the dairy herd, and when we wanted to get home quickly, we'd each grab one by the tail. The bulls would light out for the barn, their feet hitting the ground about every two yards, and ours in proportion. But the really entrancing thing was the forest that surrounded us: mountains filled with game, and trout streams loaded with fish." Jim's first book was *Forest Patrol*, based on the wilderness experiences of himself and his brother, a forest ranger. *Big Red, Irish Red* and *Outlaw Red* are dog stories about Irish setters. His other books about dogs are *Stormy, Lion Hound, Desert Dog* and *Snow Dog*.

Juv.
PZ
10.3
.K643
Sto
2001

Lebanon Valley College
Bishop Library
Annville, PA 17003

GAYLORD RG